BUMBLE HUMBLESTONE ™
AND THE SECRET CARGO

ISBN: 978-0-578-69647-8 (paperback)

Library of Congress Control Number: 2020909012

Any references to historical events, real people (specifically, Winston Churchill), or real places (specifically, The Churchill War Rooms) are productions of the author's imagination.

Front cover image, book design & illustrations by:
Sam De Santo

Printed in The United States of America

First Printing, 2020.

S&G Studios, Inc.

www.bumblehumblestone.com

BUMBLE HUMBLESTONE ™
AND THE SECRET CARGO

Written and Illustrated by

Sam De Santo

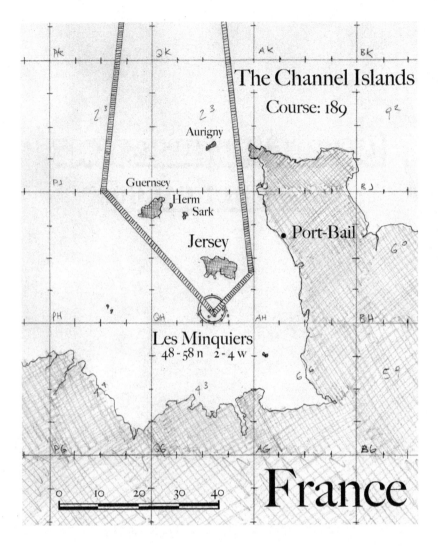

Flight path for *Operation: Mercury* – July 1942

CONTENTS

A Bad Day For Bumble

It was a quarter past six in the morning when the emergency siren blasted from tower control. Bumble Humblestone was already up and hard at work digging out the treads on a stack of dirty spare tires when he saw the distress flare fired from the cockpit of *Ace's High*. His fur stood on end.

Fibblejibbits! That plane is going to crash he thought, then jumped off the tires, grabbed his gear and started running.

"Chief! Stop sniffing! We're in trouble!" he yelled as the plane roared overhead. Chief burst out of the nearby bushes and squatted down for Bumble to climb up his leg and grab a hold of his collar. "Ready?" Chief shouted. His tiny friend nodded and they took off in hot pursuit.

From their view under the plane, they could see the left landing gear hadn't lowered and she'd have to make an emergency landing on one wheel.

"That plane is going to crash…" said Chief.

"That's just what *I* was thinking."

"But my Person is in there…"

"If anyone can get her down in one piece, it's him - now hurry!"

The plane raced down the runway and they followed as fast as they could. The right wheel inched down…closer…and closer…until it touched down.

"Here we go!" Bumble yelled.

The single landing gear creaked and groaned under the full weight of the plane. After a few seconds, the gear snapped, and *Ace's High* crashed down hard.

Sparks flew in all directions as the plane screamed down the runway, out of control. It careened off course into the mud, which splattered everywhere. Bumble frowned and shook his head as a big glob hit him right in the face and dribbled down into his jumpsuit.

"AAARRRG!"

He hated getting dirty and Chief knew it.

"Bullseye! Right in the teeth!"

"Not funny!"

After a few more yards (and a lot more mud), the plane finally slid to a complete stop, and then, all was quiet.

Bumble began wiping the mud off his face. "All's well that lands well…"

"But they crashed."

"Mmm-hmmm." Bumble reached around his collar and flicked more mud to the ground.

The cargo door opened and out jumped Captain Davenport. Smiling from ear to ear, he gave the thumbs-up signal that everything was okay. Chief barked happily, seeing that his Person was safe. Next out was the co-pilot, Eugene "Crash" McCormick. He leaned against the door, wiped his forehead with a shaking hand and drank a deep, grateful glug of water from his canteen. Last was Victor Wiesnewski, the navigator and radio operator, who stumbled out in relief and collapsed into the mud with a splash. Davenport and Crash each grabbed an arm, picked him up and started walking him towards tower control.

Happy as he was that the men were safe, Bumble looked at *Ace's High* with a lump in his throat. To him, there had now been *too* many accidents at Station 102 for them to all really *be* accidents, and the timing of this morning's crash could not have been worse. Later tonight, he and all the rest of the mice had to report to the Monthly Meeting. The Leak and Puddle Patrol, Nuts and Bolts Retrieval and Tire Tread Task Force units were all going to be lectured by Inspector Baxter, the Head Mouse, who always went out of his way to find something, anything wrong with their work. All of this made Bumble very nervous. He had a nose for trouble, and it was tingling. And unfortunately for him, his nose was almost always right.

Chief sniffed around the outside of the wreck while Bumble got a better look at the damage. What a mess! The landing gear was crushed under the belly. The propeller blades were badly bent and the engines looked cracked. Chief gave the cargo door a nudge with his nose, and they jumped inside.

Bumble looked up the length of the main cargo hold and felt even smaller than usual. "I feel like I've been swallowed by a whale!" he squeaked. His tiny voice echoed in the massive empty space.

They made their way up to the cockpit. Bumble jumped onto the control pedestal to get a better look at all of the levers, dials, switches and buttons spread across the instrument panel. He found what he was looking for right away.

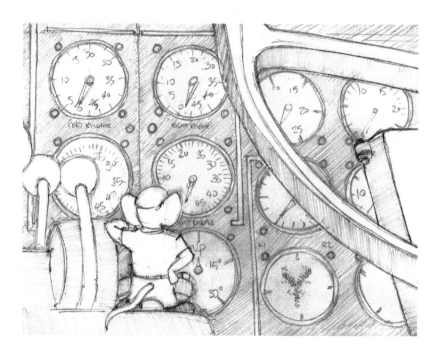

The Landing Gear Dial and the Hydraulic System Dial were both down to zero. Bumble guessed that somewhere a hose must have split or burst, and as a result, the pressurized hydraulic liquid didn't get to the left (port) side landing gear as it should have. Without hydraulic fluid, the landing gear didn't lower, and the plane crashed. Bumble scratched his chin.

"Hmmm. Very interesting," he said. "Okay Chief, we're done up here."

Chief carried Bumble out of *Ace's High* and down to the grass, much to his relief.

"Well Chief, this crash may not have been an accident." he said confidently. "There's one more thing we need to check to be 100% sure."

"But my Person saved the plane!"

"Well, that may be true, but I think someone around here is up to no good. Someone who *knows* how to be up to no good is up to no good. And that is *not* good. There's a mole at Station 102, so we need to be very careful."

"I resent that!" came a voice.

Out of the ground popped Mortimer. Mortimer was a mole, and a fussy and difficult one at that.

"Of course there's a mole at the base! You're looking at him! Me!" he thumped his thumb against his chest.

"Hi Mortimer..." Bumble and Chief sighed together. This could take some time. Once Mortimer started talking, minutes felt like hours, and the only way to end it was to agree with him and let him finish, no matter what he said.

"We of course meant 'mole' in the deep-undercover-secret-agent-sense you understand, not the biological-mammal sense..." Bumble said delicately, but Mortimer wasn't listening.

"All these accidents at the base – they're not my fault. Might be a mole doing it, but not *this* mole. No way! And why do they say 'mole' anyway? It's narrow-minded – and borderline discrimination – if you ask me!"

Bumble had an idea. Mortimer could actually be of help.

"Listen Mort. We need a favor. Need you to do some digging." He pointed at the right (starboard) wing. "Can you dig under that engine, take a peek at the wheel well? What we're looking for -"

"I'm on it! Be right back!" interrupted Mortimer. He disappeared into his hole and started digging. Chief was amazed, and Bumble smiled.

"Sometimes, all anyone needs is a job to do and they perk right up. Mortimer will tell us if the hydraulic connector rings are in place. My guess is no."

"How do you know so much about airplanes?" asked Chief.

"I think I've read every safety and repair manual we've got here, cover to cover. Some more than once. I've been dreaming about flying my whole life."

"Then why are you just working on tires?" The question stopped Bumble cold. He sighed.

"Long story. Or maybe it's a short one. I don't know. It's me. I give up too easily, always have. Whatever my dreams of doing something important might have been, here I am, on the ground, just working on tires, and that's that. End of story." He sighed again.

Chief looked his friend square in the eye.

"You know, all anyone needs is a little adventure now and then and they perk right up," said Chief. "You said it yourself. If it applies to others, it has to apply to you too."

Bumble smiled. Good old Chief.

"Thanks Pal. You're right. I guess it can't rain every day, can it?"

"But it's not raining."

"It's only a figure of speech."

Just then Mortimer popped back up. "Who said anything about rain? It's dry as a bone today! Anyway, I got under the wheel well just like you said. Horrible mess." Bumble snapped out of it.

"Did you see anything? Like a connector ring? Were the hydraulic hoses intact? Were there any -" Mortimer interrupted again.

"Hey, hey, hold on. Like I said, it's a mess. I'm no mechanic. You want to take a look? Follow me!" Back into the hole he went. Bumble gulped. Chief smiled.

"Your adventure begins…"

Bumble took a deep breath and jumped in. Up ahead, Mortimer stopped to pull a slithery earthworm out of the tunnel wall.

"Want some? They're really tasty."

"No thanks."

"Your loss." Mortimer slurped the earthworm up like one giant string of spaghetti. "Mmmmmm." Then he burped. Then he farted right in Bumble's face. It was awful. They pressed on, and after what seemed like a very long time, they finally got to the end.

"Here we are."

They climbed up out of the tunnel and found themselves dead center in the wheel well. And Mortimer was right; things *were* a mess. The main hinge was twisted like a corkscrew. The struts were broken, and frayed wires dangled from above. Oil that was supposed to be in the hydraulic hoses was dripping everywhere. Then Bumble saw something that confirmed his worst fear: the main connector ring was missing from the interior wall. It had been intentionally removed. Unscrewed. Without the ring, vibrations during the course of the flight worked the hydraulic hoses loose from each other. Precious oil needed to operate the landing gear for a safe landing had poured out. Bumble shook his head.

He signaled to Mortimer that he was ready to go. This time Bumble went into the tunnel first in case Mortimer farted again. Good thing he did. He heard a few on the way back.

Climbing out of the hole and into the open air, Bumble was visibly relieved. He patted the dirt off of his jumpsuit as

Mortimer popped his head up out of the hole and Chief sat down.

"Well...I'm afraid it's sabotage. The hydraulic hose connector ring has been removed." said Bumble. "We find that ring, we find our saboteur."

"Sabotage! At our base? Unacceptable. Completely unacceptable." said Mortimer.

"Completely. Unacceptable." repeated Chief.

All three shared a worried look. The reality of their situation was beginning to sink in. In the distance, a repair team was walking towards *Ace's High* to inspect the damage. Mortimer grumbled and took off underground. Bumble saddled up on Chief and they left the wreck. Further investigation would have to wait. It was time to get back to work.

From Bad To Worse

Bumble's job as the head of the Tire Tread Task Force was to make sure that the treads on every plane's tires were clear from debris, and that they hadn't picked up any nails, tacks or anything else potentially dangerous from another airfield. And so, he and his team had to inspect *every* tire on *every* plane, on *every* flight coming and going, in and out of Station 102 *every* day. It was back-breaking, never-ending, completely thankless work.

After the crash, the rest of Bumble's day dragged on like so many others had before.

For the remainder of the morning he cleared the treads on two planes, *The Goose* and *Ready 4 Duty*, while his afternoon was ruined by a nasty surprise smeared all over the starboard wheel of *Dream Girl*. She had rolled through a puddle of fresh hot tar at a neighboring air base. The sticky mess had gotten deep into the treads and picked up all sorts of junk as a result. It was hard, sweaty work getting it clean, and Bumble wound up doing it all by himself, as the other members of the Tire Tread Task Force - Ed and Fred - were nowhere to be seen. It didn't matter. He was determined to do the best job possible, even if it meant doing it alone. But while he worked on it, he couldn't stop thinking about the crash and that missing connector ring. It bugged him all day.

Eventually, night fell at Station 102. Between the cinderblocks and under the cold pipes of the storage shed, the mice all gathered together for the dreaded Monthly Meeting. Everyone was dirty, hungry and grouchy, especially Bumble. Going to the meeting was the last thing he wanted to do.

Inside, the Head Mouse, Inspector Baxter, welcomed the group.

"Good Evening fellow mice!" he said cheerfully.

"Good evening, Sir" they all replied.

"Thank you for meeting me tonight. I will be brief as I know you haven't had your dinners yet." He unrolled a poster from under his arm and tacked it up on the wall. It read: *Safe And Sound On The Ground*, and showed a row of happy mice cleaning up the runway under a happy-looking airplane.

"Words to live by, wouldn't you say?" he asked the group. They all nodded in agreement. Except Bumble, that is, who let out a big loud yawn. He couldn't help it, that tar was so sticky and took so much work to get loose. Inspector Baxter ignored him and moved on.

"Well to be honest, I wonder if you really *are* safe and sound...after today's accident I am very concerned. Our jobs require us to do what?" He pointed at the poster and answered.

"Stay on the ground, with our noses down. Stay out of the way, every day." He raised a single finger for emphasis. "And above all, we should never, ever talk to any of the humans. Even though we've learned their language, they must never, *ever* know that we can speak it." The group all nodded, except for Bumble who crossed his arms. He didn't like what he was hearing, and his nose started tingling. If the other mice wanted to listen to these orders and follow them, that was their business, but he didn't agree. Baxter glared at Bumble's crossed arms, then continued.

"Let's take attendance." He pulled out a clipboard and pencil. "The Leak and Puddle Patrol?" Four anxious hands went up. He checked them off the list. "Nuts and Bolts Retrieval?" This time five hands went up. "Okay...who's left?" he said as he scanned the room. But he already knew.

Bumble raised his hand, along with Ed and Fred, his useless teammates. Inspector Baxter smiled a cruel *I'll-teach-Bumble-a-lesson* smile.

"Ah yes...Bumble Humblestone and the *mighty* Tire Tread Task Force."

Ed and Fred nodded sheepishly while Bumble proudly said:

"Yes Sir, that's us."

"Well, I imagine today's accident must have been very upsetting for you."

"Why do you say that?"

"Well, *Tumble Fumblestone*, one of the wheels didn't lower as it should have."

Bumble turned red. A few of the other mice snickered. Inspector Baxter continued.

"The wheels are your department, yes or no?"

"The tire treads are, yes."

"Well then, it could very well be *your* fault, *Mumble Grumblestone*, that the wheel didn't lower, and that the plane crashed."

All the mice laughed. What a terrible thing to say! Bumble's blood boiled while Ed and Fred took a step backwards in fear. Unfortunately for Bumble, being insulted, tired, hungry and irritable, he was about to say more than he probably should have.

"For the record Sir, the tire treads and the hydraulic landing gear are two completely different things and blaming us for the crash is completely unfair! So is making fun of my name! That's uncalled for."

"For the *wreck-ord*, HQ is looking to me to whip things into shape around here, and neither you nor your team are going to stop that from happening. Understood? Heads will roll if something else goes wrong around here, starting with

14

yours. I can promise you that!" The room was silent. Ed and Fred stepped forward in a mild panic.

"Ah, Sir, we're not really a team…" said Ed.

"We report to Bumble, so he's in charge, he's the one to talk to not us…" added Fred.

Bumble couldn't believe what he was hearing, but decided to take the high road.

"With all due respect, I disagree." he said quietly. He shook his head and bit his lip.

"Duly noted, moving on…" was Inspector Baxter's final reply. The discussion was over. Everyone looked at the floor, shuffled their feet and stuck their hands in their pockets.

Baxter ended the meeting with one final thought. "All of you, remember this: we are *mice*. Gravity itself keeps us on the ground. It is where we belong. Don't let your imaginations run away with you and think you can do more than you can, because you can't. You – me – all of us – we are *only mice*."

After that, everyone quietly walked to the mess hall for dinner, while Bumble wandered off on his own. He had lost his appetite.

He climbed up on the outer fence, found a comfortable post to sit on, and sat down. What a mess things were. What a terrible day! Above him, the moon rose high into the night sky and shone brightly.

Bumble sighed, shook his head and thought about it all...long into the night.

The Deception Division

Meanwhile, in the heart of London, between Parliament and the Prime Minister's office, there stood a large, ordinary-looking building called The Office of Works. Hidden deep in its basement, under solid concrete and beams of thick steel was Britain's most secret and important set of offices: The Cabinet War Rooms. Tucked safely away from the nonstop bombing raids above ground, it was here that Winston Churchill and all his heads of intelligence and planning were able to run the war, undisturbed, twenty-four hours a day, seven days a week.

Life in the War Rooms was cramped and smoky. Officers puffed on pipes and cigarettes, while their assistants carried reports from one department to the next. Switchboard operators connected calls while nearby typists typed away, and secret messages were put into capsules, loaded into tubes, and wooshed by compressed air into either the Map Room, the Communications Room or the Main Cabinet Room where all the senior officials met.

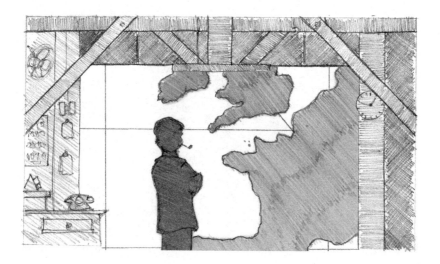

In the map room, General Fletcher was deep in thought, staring at a map of southern England, northern France and the Channel Islands scattered between them when Corporal Carruthers knocked at the door.

"Ah, Carruthers, come in," Fletcher said warmly.

"I've called you in here to explain your new assignment. You have a big day ahead of you.

"A top-secret operation to destroy the Port-Bail Bridge in occupied France has failed. Unfortunately for us and our French Resistance friends, their once-secure communications network has been broken by the Germans. As a result, nine out of ten of their secret meetings now result in capture - or worse - death. And so, the commando team we sent to blow the bridge has gone missing, and there is nothing we can to do stop a major troop and equipment train convoy scheduled to cross over it in two day's time."

Objective:
The Port-Bail Bridge
Le Pont de Port-Bail

"How does the Resistance communicate?" asked Carruthers.

"By mail.   Their phones are tapped." answered Fletcher.

"Hmmmm…"

"You will supervise the delivery of a newly built communications device to this air base here…" Fletcher pointed to Station 102 on the map and traced a line south "…and from here you will navigate the cargo's flight to a spot just below the Channel Islands for pickup. Far enough away from the French coast to avoid detection, but close enough to be within easy reach for pickup. The Resistance is counting on you and so am I, so don't let us down." Carruthers nodded "yes" but had a question.

"Sir, hasn't Station 102 been flagged with a bad accident rating? On the list of bases to be closed down?"

"Yes, they have. Lots of accidents recently. But an important mission like this should help them pull their act together, put their best foot forward, that sort of thing."

"When do we need to deliver the gadget?"

"You leave now. Let's give it a look."

Tucked away at the farthest end of the longest hallway, down a short flight of stairs into the sub-basement, was a room that didn't have a number or a name. The door made it look like a broom closet or storage room, but inside was the home of The Deception Division, and the two terribly difficult but brilliant geniuses whose job it was to come up with plans to outwit the enemy without the use of deadly force. The ideas they invented were considered so top secret, that their identities had to be protected by the use of code names. These names changed every day, sometimes a few times a day. Fletcher and Carruthers stood at the door. Carruthers cleared his throat and knocked.

"Agent Arcadia, Agent Argonaut, Command wishes to see you both."

"Arcadia and Argonaut were last week, try again," answered a voice from the other side. Carruthers pulled an index card from his pocket.

"Agents Flintlock and Forager?" he read.

"No! Now get it right or go away," answered the second voice.

"Oh, I hate these names, they were never my idea. Just open up!" Fletcher thumped on the door.

Carruthers stared at the card and racked his brain to come up with the right combination. He looked at his watch and sighed.

"Agents Backhander and Brimstone, please open the door."

To his great relief, seven locks, chains and bolts unlatched from top to bottom until the door finally swung open.

"Carruthers, you know better," scolded Backhander.

"Yes Sir, Agent Sir."

"But it's not finished yet!" yelled Brimstone.

Inside, the workspace was a complete mess. Papers were piled on the floor, blackboards were filled with scribbles, maps were stuck with pins, and bits and pieces of machinery were thrown around everywhere.

In the center of the room, the agents were putting the finishing touches on their latest masterpiece. Part telephone, part typewriter and part radio, the Top-Secret Resistance Communications Device was a very large and complicated-looking control box. It had a telephone handset on its right side, a hand crank power generator on the left and a raised typewriter keypad in the center. It had knobs and switches everywhere. Two antennas sprouted out from the back of the unit while a large radio compass dial was mounted above the center keyboard, like a single unblinking eye. No one had ever seen anything quite like it before.

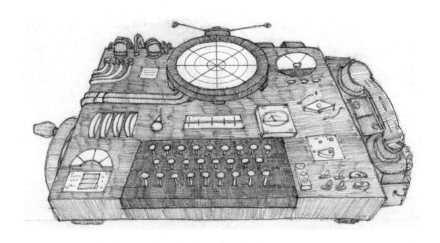

Brimstone turned the hand crank. Lights lit up. Gears started whirring to life. It almost seemed to breathe as a low and menacing hum rose from somewhere deep inside the mechanics. Backhander made one last minor adjustment to the back of the machine and gave the thumbs up signal. It was finally finished. General Fletcher was very pleased. The Agents looked on like proud parents.

"Spectacular. Brilliant. First rate." the General said.

But their moment of accomplishment was not to last. The instant they turned it off, Fletcher snapped his fingers and two soldiers wheeled a wooden transport crate into the room, along with a long metal canister on a hand truck. They leaned the canister against the wall and hefted the heavy communications device into the waiting crate. After bolting it in place and tying it down with straps, the top of the crate was nailed shut with several loud hammer strikes.

Carruthers crouched down and painted black identification numbers on the side of the crate with a set of stencils. While he did this, the Agents collected a few last-minute items to add to the canister. A standard "C" type cylinder, it stood five and a half feet tall and was filled with all sorts of supplies, from boots and blankets, to first aid kits and knives, canned food, flashlights, batteries, radios and more.

Backhander grabbed some small envelopes, pens and a thick book of French stamps from a desk drawer and placed them into the canister. Brimstone pointed to a nearby shelf.

"Don't forget the edible rice paper."

"Right! Almost did..." Backhander replied. He spoke to the soldiers as he rolled up a handful of sheets and stuck them into the canister. "If you have to eat your note, might as well make it easily digestible..."

"Tastes better than regular paper too!" added Brimstone. The soldiers closed the top of the canister and tied it down with a canvas strap.

"Gentlemen, thank you. Again, well done," said General Fletcher. The soldiers carried the crate out of the lab, while Carruthers wheeled out the canister and the General followed, closing the door behind him. The Agents locked the seven locks.

"Goodbye sweet prince. Good luck..." sighed Backhander.

"Oh, don't be so silly! Carruthers will be back."

"I was talking about the machine!"

In the hallways of the Cabinet War Rooms, everyone watched in hushed respect as the big crate made its way through the facility. The dolly squeaked as it slowly rolled along. One assistant even saluted it as it passed. The crate and canister were wheeled into a cramped elevator that slowly brought them up to street level, where a covered transport truck was waiting. The soldiers loaded everything onto the back of the truck and climbed in to guard them for the very long drive down to Station 102. Carruthers climbed behind the wheel and saluted the General.

"They did quite a job on that thingamabob..." Carruthers winced, realizing too late that he had just made a very corny rhyme.

"There's a lot more to it than meets the eye, my boy." answered the General. "We've done our part. Now, off you go. The head of Station 102 will have more instructions for you when you arrive. Good luck." The General saluted back as Carruthers put the truck into first gear and drove slowly away.

General Fletcher watched the truck disappear into the darkness, and with that, the Cabinet War Room's part of the operation was over. He went back inside to focus on the hundred other secret operations that were waiting for him.

Operation: Mercury

Early the next morning, the entire base gathered into the large Briefing Room. Big meetings of this kind were very rare at Station 102, and everyone wondered what was going on. Chief trotted around, sniffing under all the chairs but Bumble was nowhere to be seen. *He should be here...* thought Chief, and he ran out to find him.

Back at the sleeping barracks, Bumble was taking his time getting dressed. He had overslept, but a nice hot shower had done much to shake off his grogginess. After zipping up his jumpsuit, he strapped on his tool belt and pulled out his shovel. He took a long hard look at it. Would this be all he would ever get the chance to do? Was this all he was good for? Cleaning tire treads? He heaved a heavy sigh. Just then, Chief ran into the barracks and slid to a stop.

"Hey Bum!" he said.

"Hey chum." sighed Bumble.

"Something big is happening. We've got to go. The whole base is meeting."

"Good, then we can talk to Mortimer and figure out what to do. We need to find him."

"Sure, but we go to the meeting first."

"Why?"

Chief crouched down and looked his friend square in the eye. "Because it's important – and it's the right thing to do." Bumble dropped his head, beaten.

"Argh! I knew you were going to say that! Why did you have to say that?"

"You have a job to do, like it or not. So climb on. Up you go!"

As Bumble climbed up Chief's coat and grabbed a hold of his collar, Chief thought he heard the slightest protest.

"And no grumbling."

They bolted out of the barracks and ran towards the Briefing Room. As they approached, they saw Commander Hammond get out of his jeep. "Thank you Reggie. Glad someone remembers where the Briefing Room is!" he said with a wink. Philip Hammond was the base Commander, and was a cheerful man with a difficult job. It wasn't easy keeping Station 102 running properly, and thanks to the recent string of accidents, many of the men were spooked. They needed to focus their efforts, and today's news should do just that.

Chief and Bumble made it in just before the Commander, and they found a place in the back to sit and watch. As Hammond entered, the entire room shot to their feet.

"At ease! Thank you, Gentlemen. Be seated."

Everyone sat down as Hammond made his way up to the front. After a moment, complete quiet overcame the room.

"As you know, the recent string of accidents has been very bad for our reputation. So much so, that there has been actual talk of shutting us down. But fear not! Headquarters has just given us a gift. Wrapped with a big bow, in silver paper. A job we can be proud of, and something which should put Station 102 back on the map." The room erupted in applause. Bumble climbed up on top of Chief's head so he could see better, and sat between his attentive ears. This sounded good so far. He scratched Chief's head as Hammond continued.

"We have been given a front-line assignment. Highly classified. It's a first for any Air Transport Command base. HQ calls it *Operation Mercury*. For those of you without a working knowledge of Roman mythology, Mercury was the God of Messages and Communication." Hammond raised his hand. "I myself had to look it up." Everyone laughed. Hammond smiled broadly and continued.

"We are going to deliver a top-secret cargo to our friends in the French Resistance. Some sort of newly designed communications system for them to use. And we're going to do it by flying a single aircraft: in daylight, at low altitude across the English Channel, over enemy territory, and without escort. There and back again as swiftly - and safely - as possible."

"Sounds dangerous." said Bumble.

"Sounds important." said Chief.

Everyone in the room started talking. A few men raised their hands with questions.

"Why one plane, Sir?"

"Why alone?"

"Well, it's simple." Hammond replied. "If the cargo gets captured, it would be a disaster, and we can't allow that. The enemy won't be looking for a single transport plane by itself; they're too busy looking for squadrons of fighters. One C-47 flying low and fast should be able to get in and out of the target area without being detected. At least that's Headquarters' idea – and we have to prove them right."

Another hand went up. "When, Sir?"

"Ah yes…" He looked at his watch. "I'd say roughly nineteen hours from now. Probably less." An excited whisper spread across the room. "The Resistance is planning something big and they need this secret cargo immediately. So starting right now, we prepare for its arrival. This is our first, last and only mission. The future of Station 102 depends on it! Any other questions then?"

Up in the front row, Inspector Baxter turned around and eyed all the mice to make sure no one raised their hands to ask anything. Bumble frowned, crossed his arms and shook his head. Chief saw that Bumble was upset and uttered a low growl in support of his best friend.

"All right Gentlemen, that's all for now. You are dismissed. Captain Davenport, would you remain please?" The men all started heading for the exit. Bumble and Chief were closest to the door, so they ran out first.

"Did you hear that? He asked my Person to stay. My Person is going to lead the mission!" Chief said proudly.

"Yes, I bet he is. Now let's get out of here and find Mortimer!"

"On our way!" and off they went.

Captain Davenport made his way through the crowd and up to the front to greet the Commander.

"Hello Sir."

"Davenport. Have a seat."

Hammond rolled a map out on the table, and pulled several large manila envelopes from his briefcase – they were labeled "Top Secret" and each had a large red "X" crisscrossing it from corner to corner. He waited until the last man had exited the room.

"As you're top banana around here, this assignment goes to you."

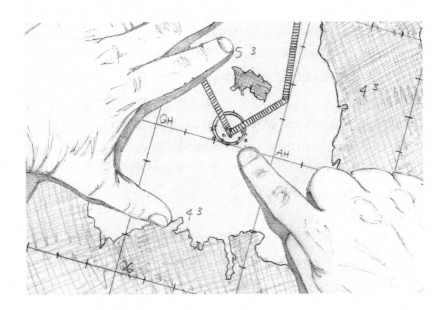

"Thank you, Sir."

"Here's the story: we can't drop this thing over mainland France, you'll get cut to pieces by anti-aircraft guns before you even reach the coast. Not to mention fighters. So it's the Channel Islands." He pointed to the map between the south coast of England and the north of France.

"Now we can't drop on any of the actual islands, as they're all occupied by Germans. However, their closeness to the French coast, and therefore our Resistance friends, makes them ideal for us now. So, we will drop here – just below the main island of Jersey, over a collection of small, uninhabited rocks called 'The Minquiers', or 'Minkies' as they're called back at HQ." He pointed to a group of tiny dots about 9 miles south of Jersey. "After you drop, a Resistance group will sail out that night and grab the crate under cover of darkness. That's the easy part. The hard part is getting you there and back again safely." Davenport smiled as he studied the map, enjoying his first big assignment. Hammond grinned and continued. "Flying over Jersey is too dangerous, so you will have to approach The Minkies this way…" His finger followed a line on the map that looped south around Jersey, down over The Minkies, then back up north across the Channel to England. "You have your choice of crew and aircraft. What you see here is for your eyes only. You can share the information with your crew once you are in the air. Until then, zip your lip. Any thoughts?" Hammond thought he had done a very good job of outlining the mission.

"Yes Sir. I'll take McCormick as my second, and Wisniewski as my navigator."

"Sorry, forgot to mention. HQ is sending a man down to baby-sit the cargo, so he'll act as navigator on this one for you. What about your plane?"

"I'd like *Eightball Charlie*, Sir."

"Really? She's an old tub!"

"Yes. But if anything were to go wrong, you'd still be left with a few good planes."

"Ah, I see. Good thinking. Alright, see to it that she's made ready." Hammond turned and started walking towards the door.

"Best of luck, and 'drop that pickle in the bucket' as they say," he concluded cheerfully. The meeting was over.

Davenport rolled up the map, collected the files and followed Hammond out the door, and the Briefing Room went back to its usual condition: empty.

Flight Map Mess

Under the shade of a parked jeep, Bumble finished recapping the briefing for Mortimer.

"...the secret cargo arrives today - and leaves first thing tomorrow - so there is very little time. Not only is it our most important mission ever, but if we fail, they are going to close us down."

"That's bad news." said Chief. Mortimer grunted in agreement.

"I think it may be worse than that Old Buddy," said Bumble. "The Resistance is urgently expecting a communications device from this base, and this base has a saboteur. Their secret cargo may be in great danger. We need to make contact with them and warn them, give them some kind of information that can help. Try to tip our odds towards success."

"But how?" asked Chief.

"I know what to do!" exclaimed Mortimer.

"Yes?" asked Bumble and Chief.

"There's an underground network we can use, to send word ahead."

"Underground?" asked Chief.

"Well of course it's underground! But it's not *actually* underground..." Mortimer pointed to the hole. "You know what I mean!" Bumble and Chief smiled. They knew what he meant.

"You two knuckleheads find that helpful piece of information we're going to send ahead, and I'll set up the delivery. Give me a little time. I know someone who can do it." Mortimer disappeared back into the hole. Bumble looked at Chief and shrugged.

"Knuckleheads?"

They were going to need a lot of help. Bumble saddled up on Chief and they ran off towards Davenport's sleeping quarters. If anyone could help, he would be the one.

Chief scratched at the door. No answer.

"Well, he's probably doing something important. He *is* leading the mission you know." Chief said proudly.

"Yes, I remember." Bumble rolled his eyes. Chief trotted over to the window and got up on his hind legs to peek inside.

"Nope. No one's home." He saw lots of files and a large map rolled out over the desk. "Looks like mission stuff on the table. We should get a look at those. Might be helpful."

He trotted back to the door. Bumble climbed up between Chief's ears and stuck his arm into the keyhole. He felt around.

"Locked. No chance we're getting in this way."

Chief thought of something.

"There's a small hole in the floorboard in the back corner of the room. My Person uses it for golf putting practice. Maybe you can get in that way. Then open the door from the inside and let me in." They trotted around to the back corner of the building and Chief showed Bumble a big crack in the foundation. "It's right about here I'd say." Bumble took the shovel from his tool belt and started chipping away at the crack.

Luckily for him, the concrete started flaking off immediately. As he worked, he became flustered.

"Are you sure we should be breaking into your Person's quarters? I've never broken the law and I'm pretty sure this is against the law."

"Against the law?! We're just unlocking a door and taking a look around. Plus, I live here, so I officially give you permission to enter. What's the matter with you anyway?"

"I don't know. Everything, I guess. The secret cargo, the Resistance, the saboteur. These are big human problems. I'm just a mouse. What can I possibly do to make a difference?" With a last big swing, Bumble broke a small hole through the foundation. He hooked the shovel back into his tool belt.

"What can you do? I'll tell you what you can do. You can get in there and take a look at the stuff on that desk. One little piece of information is all we need. We'll send it ahead and you can go back to washing wheels."

"Tire treads."

"Whatever. In you go." Bumble climbed inside.

The dark crawlspace under the floorboards was bursting with golf balls. How much putting did Davenport do? The hole in the floor above was just beyond his reach. He climbed up on a golf ball, wobbled, lost his balance and fell on his face. Chief peeked in from the hole in the concrete.

"What's taking so long?"

"Oh be quiet, you! I'm working on it!"

Bumble climbed on another ball, and pulled his shovel from his tool belt. He swung it up and hooked it into the side of the hole, grabbed a hold and pulled himself up.

"I'm in!" he yelled. Chief ran to the window to watch as Bumble scanned the small room. Under the window was a standard issue sleeping cot, complete with an itchy wool blanket and a pillow that was as flat as a pancake. A locked footlocker sat at the foot of the cot, and next to it a pair of shiny shoes. Up on the desk, Bumble could see the map and a model of an old biplane. Leaning to the side of the doorframe was the golf putter. Chief's excited breath made a steamy cloud on the glass as he watched his friend climb up the table leg and onto the desk.

Bumble found himself standing on the very same map that Commander Hammond had given to Davenport. "The Channel Islands / Course 189" was written at the top, and a red square was boxed around Station 102. Bumble walked on the map and followed the flight path. It moved directly south and made its way down and over Les Minquiers, a collection of tiny dots that were circled – Bumble guessed they must be islands – and written next to them in the Commander's own handwriting were the words "The Minkies" and the numbers "48 degrees 58 minutes north by 2 degrees 4 minutes west". This was it! These were the precise coordinates for the drop! Bumble jumped up and down and pointed excitedly. Chief fogged up the window even more.

"Write it down!" Chief yelled through the glass.

Bumble looked around. Next to the chart was a stack of mission folders labeled "Top Secret" with a large red "X" criss-crossing them from corner to corner, and next to them were an inkwell, blotter and a stack of paper. He walked over the folders and tore a small corner off the top of the stack, then opened the cap of the inkwell, and using his index finger as a pen, dunked it into the ink.

He rushed back across the mission folders onto the map, and carefully scribbled down "The Minkies" and all of the complicated numbers. He was tremendously excited, and looked at the piece of paper proudly. Victory! He did it. But unfortunately for Bumble, his moment of triumph didn't last. Out of the corner of his eye, he saw something on the map that wasn't there before. He turned to get a better look. What was it? He leaned in closer. It was a smudge...a mark...a footprint...*his* footprints!

"ACK!" he gasped.

It was an unthinkable, unimaginable disaster. He looked at the bottom of his boots – they were black! He had walked across the open ink blotter! Behind him, his footprints traced a perfect path over the map and across the mission folders – tiny black ink footprints that were sure to be seen, sure to ruin the mission, and sure to seal his doom. To make matters worse, right then, Chief started barking.

"My Person's coming!" Chief howled.

"EEEK!" Bumble shrieked.

Chief ran from the window, and Bumble tried not to panic. He looked around for a place to hide. Where?? Inside the shoes by the trunk? Can't get to them – too far away. Under the map? Surely he'd be discovered. Where then? Think Bumble, think!

Outside, Chief stalled Davenport with an excited greeting, jumping up and down, and running circles around his Person. "Chief! You're in good spirits today, huh old boy? Yeah, me too. That's a good boy." Chief barked again. Hurry up Bumble!

As Davenport pulled out his keys, Bumble smacked his forehead with his inky right hand and realized where he could hide. As the keys rattled in the lock, Bumble made a mad dash for the biplane model and jumped into the open cockpit. As the door swung open, he held his breath and froze.

Davenport entered the room humming loudly and off key. He threw some papers on the cot, put a cigarette in his mouth and patted his empty shirt pockets.

Without looking he rolled up the map, grabbed the mission folders and tucked everything under his arm. He opened the desk drawer and found his lighter, then left the room as quickly as he had entered. He never even lit the cigarette he was so excited. He slapped his thigh and Chief followed him over to the Main building.

Bumble waited several seconds before letting his breath out. That was close. Outside he heard Chief barking into the distance. All clear. He shook his head. Of all the stupid clumsy things to do, Bumble could not believe he ruined the map. In his distraction, Davenport hadn't seen the footprints, but surely someone would soon.

"Fibblejibbits..." he muttered to himself as he ran off the desk and jumped into the putting hole.

6

On A Wing And A Prayer

Outside, Mortimer was waiting. He drummed his six fingers impatiently against the dirt as Bumble emerged.

"Ah! Finally! Here he is. I'll introduce you."

Bumble was startled as a beautiful white pigeon gently fluttered down next to them. She had a perky pink beak, big round eyes and was covered in flawless snow-white feathers. She looked more like a dove than a pigeon. He couldn't help but stare. She really was a pretty bird.

"Yeah, I get that a lot." she said.

"Pardon?" Bumble replied, trying to look away. He hadn't said anything.

"Everyone thinks I'm a dove. But I'm actually a pigeon. Robin's the name. Robin Winchester." She extended her wing. Bumble gripped the end of her primary feathers and shook them gently. How did she know what he was thinking?

"Um, Bumble.   Bumble Humblestone." he said, suddenly self-conscious.

"Aren't you sweet." She winked.

Bumble had never shaken feathers with a bird before, much less an aviatrix, much less an attractive one. This was certainly out of his regular routine. He could get used to meeting attractive agents on missions of top secrecy. Mortimer just shook his head. He didn't see what the big deal was.

"Alright then, introductions made. Bumble the mouse, meet Robin the bird."

"Pigeon." she corrected him.

"Alright," Mortimer sighed, "Robin the Carrier Pigeon."

"Actually I prefer 'Homing Pigeon', if you please. Difference in breeding."

"Can we proceed?! Please? Does it matter, really?" Mortimer was upset, not that it took much to get him there, but now that he was, Robin thought it best to let him get on with things. "Of course," she smiled. Mortimer motioned to Bumble to start.

"Well, Miss Winchester…" Bumble started.

"Robin." she corrected.

"Well, Robin, very soon, a top-secret cargo from this base is going to be air lifted to The French Resistance, and we animals want to make sure it gets where it's supposed to go and into the right hands. That's where you come in. These are the coordinates for the drop. Highly classified." Bumble unrolled the torn corner of paper with his messy ink-splattered handwriting and showed it to Robin: "The Minkies" / "48 degrees 58 minutes north by 2 degrees 4 minutes west". She memorized the numbers. Bumble continued. "Once you deliver this to your contacts, they'll know where to go to pick this mystery cargo up and hopefully put it to some good use. We don't know what it's going to be exactly, but we do know it's communications related." Robin looked at the piece of paper. She then looked at Bumble.

"Well that explains it." she said.

"Explains what?" asked Bumble.

"How you got that black handprint on your forehead." she smiled. Bumble was again at a loss for words, this time out of complete embarrassment. He looked at the palm of his writing hand (it was black) and wiped his brow with his other hand (it came up clean, no ink). He could only imagine what he looked like.

Robin was now all business. She took the paper, rolled it up in her talons and slipped it into a tiny canister tied to her leg. "Gentlemen, I am off."

She turned to Mortimer. "I would tell you where I am going but that information is 'need to know' and you don't need to know. Part of Confidential Pigeon Service regulations, I'm sure you understand." Mortimer grumbled. She then turned to Bumble. "However, I can tell *you*, my dear mouse, that your Pigeon-Gram will be delivered. Of that you can be certain. Intelligence gathering and distribution is what we at the CPS do best." Bumble smiled, proud that his contribution to the mission was going somewhere, even if he wasn't.

"By the way," Robin continued, "whatever you did to get this information, I'm sure you were very brave." The compliment surprised Bumble greatly.

"Thank you Miss Winchester," he said.

"Robin." she reminded him.

"Robin, yes. Be careful! And get back safe." Bumble really meant it.

41

"I'm a homing pigeon – I always come back." She winked again.

And with that, she took off, and quickly became a very small white dot in a very big sea of blue.

"Well Mortimer, we're on our way. What do you think of that?"

Mortimer was nowhere to be seen, having already burrowed back inside his hole. Bumble looked back up to the sky and smiled.

Robin headed south towards the French coast. Her objective was Saint Helier, the capital of Jersey Island, where resistance agents were already in place and waiting for her arrival. She should be there by sundown.

Robin climbed to a great height, stopped flapping and let the warm wind carry her. Her feathers rippled against the passing air. Down below the sun glistened off of the water in a million pinpoints at once. It was beautiful. Shining, shimmering and magical. Robin loved her job on days like this.

"Well, how do you like that? That cute little mouse and that dirty old mole sending me out across the Channel. On a mission to help drop a top-secret-something-or-other on 'The Minkies'? 'The Minkies'? Never heard of such a silly name for a bunch of rocks in the water..." she said to no one in particular. She didn't expect an answer. But a reply did come – from above.

Out of the sun screamed a pair of British fighters. They flashed past her at full speed to intercept a squadron of German fighters that had just come into view. It would be a duel in the sky, and Robin found herself right in the middle of it: a pigeon in a dogfight.

For her part, she did her best just to stay out of the way. There were fighters and bullets flying everywhere. One German plane buzzed right past her at 400 miles an hour, almost clipping her feathers. "WAAAAH!" she screamed, startled beyond words. She spun around in the slipstream of the passing fighter, turning upside down and right side up again, flapping madly. "Watch it!" Then a British fighter zipped past, fast on his tail. "Go get him! My hero!" she yelled.

In the distance, though, she saw trouble. An enemy fighter moved into firing position behind her hero. He would be dead in less than a minute if she didn't do something. She would have to be careful though, if she didn't want to wind up splattered on the windshield. Her attack would have to happen from a distance somehow. Wait – that was it! The windshield! That was any fighter's vulnerable spot. If only she was carrying an egg, she could lob one off and break his glass. Oh well, she would have to do the next best thing. And it wasn't going to be pretty, but this was war.

The fighters turned in her direction. She started to dive. The timing would have to be perfect. Her speed plus distance, plus their speed plus gravity, equaled a one in a million chance that her poop would hit the German's windshield at just the right angle. Good thing she had eaten those extra berries for breakfast this morning.

Here they come. It was now or never. She angled up and let it go.

"Bombs away!" she yelled.

The poop dropped. For a moment it hung and wobbled in the air. Would it work? And then, the German fighter flew right smack into it, and the turd hit a perfect bull's-eye on the glass.

It splattered all over the windshield. The pilot opened his canopy and tried to wipe it clean, but only succeeded in smearing it around and making it worse. Now he couldn't see anything, and had to break off and retreat.

"Victory! Take that!" Robin yelled.

Behind them, the remaining Germans decided to cut their losses and head back to base. The dogfight was over. Once again, everything was quiet and calm, and it was just Robin, the blue sky and the puffy clouds in the distance.

"'The Minkies' – never heard of such a silly name. *That's* for sure."

She flew peacefully away.

A Lucky Penny Always
Turns Up

Back in the main hangar, Bumble was feeling good. From up on the spare parts table, he watched as the maintenance crews worked on *Eightball Charlie*. It was very exciting. Men were crawling all over her wings, digging in her engines, checking every inch. Once they were finished, the pilot and co-pilot would then do a smaller inspection of their own, and she'd be cleared to fly.

While Bumble sat, he flipped through a deck of aircraft spotter cards that were scattered on the shelf next to him. They featured a front, side and bottom view of every aircraft from every country in black silhouette for quick identification. He looked through them every once in a while to test his knowledge. So far he was doing well. He pulled one out and looked. It was a big plane with 4 engines, a long greenhouse cockpit and twin-finned tail.

"Ah. Bomber. British. Lancaster."

He turned the card. He was right.

"Ha! Hello 'Lanc'."

He pulled another card. This plane was a small fighter with a "bubble top" cockpit. The body was thick and robust while the wings were squared off at the ends.

"Fighter. American. P-51 Mustang. 'Cadillac of the Skies'."

He turned it over. Right again.

"Two for two!"

As he pulled another card, Davenport entered the hangar and walked right past the spare parts table. "Hey Everyone – gather 'round," Davenport called out to the group. Work slowed. "This will just take a second." Work stopped. "I just want to say thank you. Thank you for taking care of *Eightball Charlie* for me. We're privileged to have the chance to do something truly special, and it wouldn't be possible without all of you. The old bird's got to fly better than she's ever flown before, and although she may not have the greatest reputation, I know you'll make her respectable." The men laughed. "I wish I could tell you more, but you know I can't. Bottom line? She's in for the flight of her life, and so are we! All of us! Station 102 is going to show all of them back at HQ how it's done. We're going to surprise them, that's for sure. So here's to you, the best in the business!" He took off his hat and everyone cheered. It was an excellent pep talk. Bumble clapped excitedly and smiled.

"What a guy," said a nearby voice. Bumble turned.

It was Inspector Baxter, who took one of the silhouette cards, set it under his butt and plopped down right next to him on the spare parts table. Bumble stopped clapping and put his hands in his pockets. His nose started to tingle.

"Exciting day, isn't it?" asked Inspector Baxter.

"I guess..."

"Yes, the pressure is on, I can tell you that. Big mission. A lot riding on it."

"Uhmm-hmmm..." Bumble mumbled back. He was feeling smaller by the minute. Something wasn't right. Inspector Baxter continued.

"I'm under a great deal of pressure from HQ. Being in my position can be quite the burden I must tell you." Bumble dreaded hearing what he would say next.

"You need to appreciate the position I'm in, mouse to mouse. I'm going to start at the end and work my way to the beginning. So, here it goes. I'm putting someone else in charge of the Tire Tread Task Force for this mission."

Bumble was stunned. He felt his entire chest tighten like a fist. Inspector Baxter continued. "Yesterday's crash has HQ seeing red and I need to offer you up as a peace offering to them. There will be other work for you, just not this, not now."

After a moment, Bumble swallowed hard, got himself together and again decided to take the high road. "Well, you let me know if there is anything else I can do..." he managed to choke out. Inspector Baxter got up, replaced the silhouette card on the shelf and slid down the leg of the table to the floor without saying anything more.

Bumble felt weak and tried to breathe. How could headquarters blame the Tire Tread Task Force for yesterday's accident? There was a chain of command for everything that happened on the base. He and his team were the lowest mice on the ladder, how could it be that he got singled out? HQ never bothered themselves with details like clean tire treads. Besides, the tires had nothing to do with the accident. The connector ring wasn't in the wheel well where it was supposed to be, for crying out loud! Something strange was going on, but he was the one to take the blame for this? How could this be happening?

Bumble watched as Inspector Baxter approached Ed and Fred, and told them they were now in charge of the Tire Tread Task Force. They looked very proud to be given the honor. As Inspector Baxter walked away, they caught a glimpse of Bumble up on the table. Fred turned beet red and didn't know how to react when their eyes met, and Ed dropped his head. After an awkward moment, they shrugged and walked off towards *Eightball Charlie*. This was the second time they had hurt Bumble by not coming to his defense. They were supposed to be a team. How could they just hang him out to dry? Well, it didn't really matter. They were in charge now, and that was that.

Bumble climbed down and slowly made his way across the hangar, away from all the activity, toward a small hole in the wall. Tacked on the wall above the hole was a big poster of Winston Churchill, his expression very serious and full of strength. It read: "DESERVE VICTORY!".

Bumble stood and looked at the poster for a good long time. He felt as if Churchill was staring down at him, pointing right into his very soul. Deserve Victory indeed. He walked into the dark little hole in the wall and never felt smaller or more alone.

Meanwhile, Crash finished up a systems check in *Eightball Charlie*'s cockpit. Davenport climbed in and clapped him on the shoulder.

"How we lookin'?"

"Good. Really good."

"We should have these top-secret missions all the time. We could get used to this, huh Crash?"

"Yep. Not too shabby." Crash grinned. He had to admit, it was nice that the plane was finally getting the attention she needed.

"Okay, I'll see you in the morning. Try to get some sleep while you can. *Operation Mercury* is almost here!"

Davenport clapped him on the shoulder again and left the cockpit. Crash was glad to see his Captain was in good spirits, but privately, Crash was nervous about the mission. They could be flying over enemy territory, and might get shot at, which was not at all what he signed up for at Air Transport Command. Delivery flights between friendly bases were one thing, but dangerous secret missions were something else.

Crash glanced at the instruments one last time. Everything looked good, and the cockpit was peaceful and quiet. In a few hours it would be a very different story in here, but for now, he enjoyed this brief moment of calm.

He reached into his pants pocket and pulled out his lucky penny. He flipped it in the air, caught it and squeezed it tightly in his hand. He was going to need all the help he could get tomorrow. They all did. The moment of quiet passed, and it was time for Crash to go.

He left the cockpit, marched down the empty cargo hold and jumped out of *Eightball Charlie*'s main doors. As he did, he couldn't see that Smiley Reilly, the never-happy-always-frowning mechanic, was passing under the plane at exactly the same moment, pushing a handcart full of spare wiring. They bumped into each other, and Crash landed on the concrete floor. He saw stars.

"Hey! You all right?" asked Smiley. A few of the other mechanics quickly gathered around.

"Yep I'll live…" groaned Crash.

"Okay then. Give you a hand?"

"Sure." answered Crash. Smiley and the other mechanics set their tools down and started clapping, giving Crash a round of applause for his elegant fall from the plane. They were a tough crowd.

"Very funny." moaned Crash.

"Just kiddin'." Smiley extended his hand and Crash took it and stood up. He was a little woozy. "How's your melon?" asked Smiley.

"Still attached."

"Okay then. Watch where you're jumpin' next time." Smiley pushed his cart of wires, while Crash rubbed the back of his head and felt around. He looked at his hand, and luckily there was no blood on it, but there was no penny in it either! Crash patted his pants pocket. Nothing. He looked around. No coin. Crash was suddenly very upset. His lucky penny! He couldn't fly tomorrow's mission without it. He crouched down and started looking around.

The penny had flown from his hand, landed on its edge and had started rolling across the hangar. It rolled and rolled and rolled – like it was on a mission – and finally found its way into the small hole under the "Deserve Victory" poster. It spun, wobbled and flattened out right next to Bumble. It shimmered and shined while a desperate voice shouted in the distance.

"Has anyone seen my lucky penny? *Anyone?!*"

Bumble looked out of the hole to see Crash, crawling around on all fours, looking under gas cans, boxes and spare parts. He was white as a sheet and made a huge racket. Poor guy. Looked like Bumble wasn't the only one having a bad day. Bumble picked up the penny and walked out of the hole, splashed into a big puddle of oil (where was The Leak and Puddle Patrol?) put his fingers in his mouth and whistled. That stopped Crash in his tracks. He looked up, looked behind, and finally looked down to see Bumble, holding up the coin with a big smile. Crash gasped.

"AHHHH! I don't believe it! Oh thank you, thank you, thank you!" He crawled over, sat down next to Bumble, and Bumble handed him the coin. He squeezed it tightly. Color came back into his face, his breathing slowed and he started to calm down.

"You don't know what a big thing you just did...everyone around here thinks I'm nuts for carrying this, but I have my reasons!" said Crash.

Bumble smiled again. It was nice to get the focus off of himself and see someone else happy. Helping someone else was always a good thing to do when he was feeling down, and it usually helped him to cheer up. But not today. His smile faded into a look of sadness and worry, and he sighed.

Crash could see Bumble was upset, and wanted to do something nice for this little mouse. "You know, when I have a bad day, one thing that I find helps to clear the head is to focus on the stomach. And I know just the thing. How would you like a little cheese?" Bumble lit up. He squeaked in agreement.

"Well then, let's have ourselves a walk over to the mess hall. I'm friends with the cook, and I'm sure he can find something for us. Deal?" Bumble nodded. Crash offered his hand and Bumble jumped on.

Crash put him in his front shirt pocket so he could see where they were going. The promise of cheese was already helping Bumble forget about that nasty Inspector Baxter. He and Crash strode out of the maintenance hangar and into the fresh air. This sure was better than sitting in a dark little hole in the wall.

The sun was beginning to set. Beautiful reds and violets were creeping across the sky. He thought of Robin Winchester and wondered where she was, and how she was doing.

The Walnut Brigade

With the dangers of the English Channel finally behind her, Robin flew peacefully along the Jersey Island coastline. What a relief to be over dry land, even if it was occupied by the enemy. The sun was setting beautifully in the west, she was on schedule and close to completing her part of the operation.

All that was left to do now was to hand the coordinates off to the next set of agents. Four times each day, all across Europe – at sunrise, noon, sunset and midnight - agents of every species met at public landmarks for spy duty. If an animal had information or knew something important that needed to be passed on, a fellow agent would be waiting at the local town square, fountain, statue, cathedral and so on. That's how Mortimer had found Robin, and that's how Robin was going to find the Pasetti Brothers.

She turned and flew inland, over the coastal defenses, past marshes and fields and finally into the small township of Saint Helier, the capital of Jersey. She passed the church spire and flew over to the main town square. Smack in the middle of the square stood a tall monument, an obelisk, surrounded by water fountains, benches and a few trees. That *had* to be the meeting point. She landed on the very tip-top of the obelisk and waited.

Down below, the square was busy with all sorts of activity. Old ladies in headscarves shuffled from the bakery to the vegetable stands, anxious to buy what they needed before it became dark, while small packs of German soldiers patrolled the area. Officers sat at an outdoor café drinking espresso in little cups and smoking filter-less cigarettes. Their black Mercedes-Benz staff car was parked near the fountains, with a bored driver sitting behind the wheel staring into space.

The sky turned purple as it got a little darker. Robin kept looking. After a few minutes her contacts finally arrived: three squirrels, who quickly ran in single file down a side street, froze at the corner, dashed across the square, then scrambled under a truck and surfaced at the fountain, sitting on one of the benches, their big bushy tails twitching in excitement. The littlest one of them held a big walnut in his little hands. The Pasetti Brothers had arrived.

Born from a well-to-do, almost aristocratic Northern Italian family, the brothers left home at the start of the war to escape the Fascists and find adventure. The oldest, Alessandro, was thoughtful and responsible, and took care of his brothers as best he could. He was a good brother and a good leader, and his brothers loved and respected him very much. Nicolo, the middle brother, was the crafty one, and could be counted on for getting them in and out of tight spots alive. Where he got his dangerous streak from no one knew, but it had come in handy on more than one occasion. The youngest of the three was Eduardo. He had a hard time keeping up with his older brothers, not because they were especially fast, or because he was especially slow, but because he was always stopping to eat. His appetite was uncontrollable. Nuts, berries, seeds, and mushrooms were everywhere this time of year, much to Eduardo's delight, and much to his brothers' irritation. When they joined the underground, the brothers Americanized their names to keep the authorities off their tails, so they became known as Alex, Nicky and Edward. Robin flew down to meet them.

"Hello Boys."

The brothers stopped twitching and froze, as if their stillness would somehow make them invisible. Robin began the briefing. "I've got some information that needs to be passed along as soon as possible, priority one." She paused, but there was no reaction – the brothers remained frozen. Out of the corner of his mouth Alex murmured "…password…"

"Oh, right! Password! Silly me." She cleared her throat and quietly asked, "Why did the cow jump over the moon?"

"To get to the other side." replied Alex.

"Knick knack paddy whack…" she continued.

"E – I – E – I – O." he concluded.

Satisfied that she had passed security procedure, the squirrels sprang to life and introductions were made.

"I'm Alex."

"I'm Nicky."

"I'm Edward."

"Brilliant! I'm Robin. Now – on to business." She reached down to the tube attached to her leg and pulled out Bumble's little piece of paper. "These are the drop coordinates for a top-secret cargo flying in from England for the Resistance. Not exactly sure when, not exactly sure what, but it's soon and it's communications related." She handed the paper to Alex. He unrolled it and memorized the coordinates. "You boys have got to get these coordinates to your contacts, and make sure the cargo gets into the right hands."

Edward passed the big walnut to Nicky, who turned a tiny latch on the shell. The walnut popped open on little hinges to reveal that the inside was completely hollowed out and empty! Alex tucked the paper inside, Nicky closed it up and Edward closed the tiny latch. It looked like a walnut again. No one would ever suspect they were carrying secret information – it was a perfectly simple disguise. After all, they were squirrels carrying a nut. What could be more natural than that? They smiled a mischievous smile and prepared to go on their way.

"I'm impressed." said Robin.

"Thank you, Miss Robin. We'll take it from here." said Alex. The brothers all saluted.

"Goodbye, Miss Robin." said Nicky.

"You sure are a pretty dove." said Edward. She smiled and patted him on his head with her feathers. No need to correct him.

"Thank you, Love. Good luck boys!" She waved to the brothers as they ran across the plaza and out of sight. And with that, Robin Winchester's part of the operation was done. She flew up into the darkening sky, ready for whatever new adventure tomorrow would bring.

The brothers' target, meanwhile, was The Red Lion, an old tavern on the outside of town. Its second-floor storage attic was the secret hideout of a group of French Resistance rats called The Rodents of Rouen. Anything Resistance-related had to go through them. They were a tough and nasty bunch, and didn't even have the decency to consider their squirrel cousins part of the rodent family, which they were. Neither did they consider any of the woodchucks, porcupines or gophers that had also helped them out from time to time as being rodents either. But war changes everything, and everyone had to pull together for the common good, so their snobby attitudes were put up with. For the time being. The Pasetti Brothers had bigger problems to overcome.

Breaking into The Red Lion would not be easy. Now that it was nighttime, the roads all over town would be overrun with patrols and the tavern itself would be overflowing with German soldiers. Many squirrel agents had met their doom under the wheels of fast-moving German vehicles, while others had found themselves the unfortunate object of target practice by drunken German soldiers. Their time in The Red Lion would have to be quick, but first, they had to get there in one piece.

Alex took the lead while Nicky carried the walnut and Edward followed closely behind. They ran in single file across a cobblestone street and narrowly missed getting run over by a six-wheeled German "Boxer" lightweight truck. Six wheels! What a dreadful truck – so many ways to get squashed! They climbed up a storm drain on the roof of an old antique shop to plan their next move. The tavern was due north, and a good distance away. Alex and Nicky studied the streets below, while Edward found some old acorns in the roof's rain gutter, sat down and started snacking.

"Any ideas?" asked Alex.

"I think we need to hitch a ride." answered Nicky.

"I agree. Now that it's dark, we're going to get squashed. But let's find something with four wheels this time and not six."

"How about three?"

Nicky pointed to a motorcycle parked far up the street. It had a sidecar, which would be the perfect hiding place for the squirrels.

"Fantastic! Off we go!" said Alex excitedly. Nicky grabbed the walnut, and he and Alex started climbing down the opposite side of the roof. As they got about halfway, they realized Edward was not with them, so they climbed back up and saw him just sitting there, happily munching on the acorns he had pulled from the rain gutter. They looked at each other and rolled their eyes.

"Edward, stop eating!" they both yelled.

Edward turned around and waved. He got up, brushed off a few bits of acorn shell, and trotted over to their side of the roof. All three brothers then climbed down to the street and started running. They were in luck – a soldier was approaching the motorcycle – but they had better get a move on if they wanted to hitch a ride. They ran as fast as they could. The soldier climbed onto the motorcycle, stood on the starter and the engine sputtered to life just as the squirrels reached the sidecar. Nicky jumped in first, followed by Edward, who slipped and fell. The soldier adjusted his goggles and slipped his gloves on. He was almost ready to drive off. Alex gave Edward a big shove from behind and Nicky extended his hand. Edward's back feet scratched and scraped against the sidecar, but Nicky got a hold of him and pulled him up. He was in. Now it was Alex's turn. The soldier turned the throttle, revved the engine and put the motorcycle into gear. It started to move! Alex ran along the sidecar and frantically tried to get a grip, but missed. The soldier opened the throttle and motorcycle started to speed up – it was now or never. With all his might, Alex jumped and caught a hold of the spare wheel on the back of the sidecar – he gripped the spokes in the center of the wheel and held on for dear life. As the motorcycle bounced over a long series of cobblestones, Alex's grip began to slip.

"Hold this!" Nicky handed Edward the walnut and scrambled over the tire to offer his brother a hand. Just as the motorcycle picked up speed, Nicky pulled Alex up to safety.

That was close. All three sat on the sidecar seat cushion, relieved. After a moment, Edward tapped Alex's shoulder.

"What if we don't turn north?" he asked.

"Hadn't thought of that..." Alex answered sheepishly.

If they turned south, they would have gone through all that running, climbing and pulling for nothing. What to do? Nicky had an idea. He looked up at the soldier, wiggled his fingers, then squeezed his eyes shut.

"Left. Left. Left." he repeated. The soldier didn't see him and certainly couldn't hear him, but a little mind control couldn't hurt. They had a 50-50 chance of him turning in the right direction, so why not try to tip the odds in their favor? Alex and Edward joined in.

"Left. Left. Left." they all repeated as the motorcycle reached the intersection. The soldier stopped the bike and looked both ways. Several German trucks drove by.

"Left. Left. Left." They all wiggled their fingers in mind-control effort. After the trucks passed and the intersection was clear, the soldier put the bike in gear and turned...left.

"Victory!" the brothers yelled. The motorcycle picked up speed and they headed north towards the tavern. The mind control worked!

"Just like we planned." said Alex proudly.

"Without a hitch, without a glitch. We know which way is which, don't we big brother?" said Nicky. The brothers relaxed and enjoyed their ride in the open sidecar as the wind blew through their fur. They would arrive at the tavern in no time. Edward looked at the walnut.

"Holding this thing is making me hungry." he said.

"Edward, stop eating..." said Alex.

"I'm not eating, I'm just *thinking* about eating." Edward sighed.

They drove on, and after a short while, The Red Lion became visible up ahead. The light from the tavern windows was warm, golden and very inviting. Music and voices grew louder as they drove closer. German military trucks of every sort were parked outside. As they approached, they got ready to jump off, but to their delight, the motorcycle slowed down, turned into the tavern's parking lot and pulled up next to one of the trucks. The brothers looked at each other in amazement. What were the chances of that? This had been a good mission so far. They jumped out of the sidecar and ran over to the closest tree. Now for the hard part – getting into the tavern and getting up to the second-floor attic safely, without being seen, caught or shot.

The front entrance was clogged with drunken soldiers. Several stood in the doorway smoking and talking. Others stumbled out and leaned against the trucks to get some fresh air. A few laid down in the dirt to keep the world from spinning any faster.

"Can't get in that way." said Alex.

Nicky pointed to a small second story window above the tavern sign. It was cracked open.

"There." said Nicky.

Alex nodded and looked up at the tree above them. Its biggest branch was also its longest, and it looked close enough to make the jump to the roof. It was worth a shot. Alex started climbing. Nicky gripped the walnut in his teeth and followed, while Edward again followed from behind. They scratched their way around the trunk and up to the big branch. Then, as quietly and as carefully as possible, they crawled out onto the limb. It was dark and very hard to see where they were going. Every step brought them further out over the trucks and over the soldiers, but closer to the tavern. Edward tried not to look down. Alex got to the end of the branch and judged the distance. It looked good.

He backed up a few steps, ran and jumped – and just made it onto the top of the bracket holding the Red Lion sign. He climbed down onto the roof shingles and waved for the next brother. Nicky motioned to Edward.

"Your turn squirt."

Edward looked scared. Nicky encouraged him.

"You can do it! Ready? Go!"

Edward ran and jumped – and missed the bracket. He hit the sign with a loud WHUMP and fell on the roof with a CLUNK. The sign swung from the impact, and the soldiers looked up to see what the noise was. Alex and Edward remained perfectly still. The soldiers didn't see them and turned back to their conversations. That was close. The brothers needed to move fast. Nicky backed up, clamped down hard on the walnut with his teeth and jumped. He flew gracefully through the air and made it to the bracket, but at the last second lost his balance, and the walnut flew out of his mouth. It clattered into the rain gutter and started rolling towards the downspout!

Alex stared in surprise as Edward sprang into action, ran alongside the gutter and caught the walnut just before it disappeared. Alex and Nicky gave their little brother the thumbs up. Edward held on to the walnut proudly as they all climbed into the open window.

They were halfway there.

Into The Lion's Den

The Main Room was a big open area. They found themselves up in the balcony seating on the second floor. A large circular cast iron chandelier hung from heavy chains out into the center of the space. Directly below it was an enormous round wooden bar surrounded by tables and stools. Booths lined the far walls. Piano music came from somewhere down there too.

The tavern was jammed with German soldiers, all shouting, singing, drinking and smoking. They covered every square inch of the place – there was no room to move – boots were everywhere. The noise was incredible, and the air was thick with smoke and smelled of stale beer. It was like a bad dream. Alex, Nicky and Edward weighed their options.

"We'll have to stay above the ground floor." Alex stated matter-of-factly.

"Agreed." said Nicky.

"Huh?" said Edward, a bit scared.

"Look, there it is." Alex pointed directly across the great space to the other side of the room. It was the storage attic. It had a little door and a ladder was propped up below it. Inside, presumably, waited the Rodents of Rouen. Their objective was finally within sight. Now, how to get there?

The tavern had a beautiful old-fashioned cathedral ceiling – long wooden beams crisscrossed the length of the room. Nicky studied the beams while Edward again tried not to look down.

"We'll have to use the beams under the rafters. Get across the space that way. Stay as high and as far away from these guys as possible." said Nicky.

"Agreed." said Alex.

"Huh?" asked Edward, more scared.

"Don't worry squirt..." assured Nicky. "Up we go."

As they started their climb up to the rafters, the sounds of semi-organized drunken singing began to boom through the tavern with "Schnitzelbank", a traditional German children's friendship song. Off-key, off-time and very loud, the soldiers began the long "accumulation" song, with each verse adding to the next.

"IST DAST NICHT EINE SCHNITZELBANK?"

"JA, DAS IST EINE SCHNITZELBANK!"

Every time the soldiers sang the word "Schnitzelbank", they slammed their beer mugs and stomped their feet, causing the whole place to shake like an earthquake. For the Pasetti Brothers, it was an unwelcome twist to an already difficult situation. If they knew the song, they could plan for when the thumps and stomps would come, but since they never heard it before, they were thrown off balance again and again as they crept along the skinny beams high above. Edward wished he had handed the walnut to Nicky but it was too late now to do anything about it. They had to get across the room, no matter what was happening below.

After some creeping and crawling, stomping and more thumping, the brothers had gotten about halfway across the room when the walnut suddenly flew out of Edward's grip. The brothers watched in horror as the walnut drifted through the air. It dropped to the balcony, bounced off a table, and flew down to the circular bar far below, where it plunged right into a bowl of mixed nuts! The brothers gasped. Soldiers were eating those nuts! If one of them picked up their nut by mistake, the whole operation would be blown! A nightmare! They had to act fast.

Alex led the way, and crawled upside down along one of the rafters. When he got to the center of the room, he let go, caught the chandelier and looked down to the circular bar below. There were a lot of bowls with a lot of nuts, and he was no longer sure which bowl was theirs. They all looked the same! He motioned for his brothers to follow. Nicky dropped down next to him.

"Which one? Which bowl?" Alex asked, slightly panicked.

"*You* don't know? *I* don't know!" Nicky yelled.

"Well I don't know either!" Alex snapped back.

"I do..." said Edward, as he carefully climbed down the chain to the center column. "It's that one." He pointed. "Right there..."

"Which one?" Alex asked again. Edward leaned forward and pointed with urgency.

"Thaaaaaat – " Edward lost his grip, cartwheeled through the air and fell smack into one of the bowls. Nuts splashed everywhere. Soldiers jumped in surprise.

"AHH! EICHHORNCHEN!" they yelled, ("squirrel!"). The mission, that had started out so well, and had gone so smoothly, was now falling apart. One soldier pulled an enormous knife and stabbed it down into the bar, narrowly missing Edward. Another soldier made a grab for Edward but missed, and instead knocked over yet *another* bowl of nuts, which fell to the floor and spread in every direction. The soldier with the knife prepared to take another stab at Edward. Down the length of the bar, three bowls away, Edward saw a fat soldier grab their walnut and reach for a nutcracker. He shrieked frantically to his brothers and pointed.

"That's it! That's it! Three bowls down!"

Alex and Nicky zeroed in and prepared to jump. Edward leaped off the bar as the soldier with the knife took another stab at him and missed. He hit the floor and ran towards the fat soldier with the nutcracker. Alex and Nicky jumped from the chandelier. Alex miscalculated and landed in a tall mug of beer, while Nicky landed on another soldier's head. The soldier panicked and knocked Nicky to the ground. The bartender pulled out a pistol and started yelling for order in the bar, but no one listened.

Edward ran at full speed – over, under and in between all the boots that were everywhere. The fat soldier with the nutcracker prepared to break the walnut, when he felt something crawl up his leg – it was Edward! He dropped the nut and the nutcracker, and screeched. The other soldiers around him all pointed and laughed. Then, to his amazement, Alex, dripping wet with beer, walked up, grabbed the walnut, and jumped off the bar. The fat soldier pushed his beer away, and decided he had had too many, and must be seeing things.

Nicky ran towards the ladder and started climbing. Edward grabbed a few stray nuts up off the floor. Alex followed. Soldiers all around were in a state of confusion. The brothers got to the top of the ladder and frantically banged on the door to the storage attic. Their banging cracked it open just enough for them to fit inside. As they closed the door behind them, a bottle thrown from below smashed against it. They had made it by the skin of their teeth.

Inside the attic, the brothers panted and tried to catch their breath. As their eyes adjusted to the darkness, they saw that they were not alone. In front of them sat four black rats calmly playing cards at a small table. Their faces were weather-beaten and rough, marked with deep scars and recent scratches from the dangerous lives they led. They hardly even looked up at the squirrels. So these were The Rodents of Rouen. Alex made the introduction.

"The Pasetti Brothers, at your service." Alex did his best to look official, even though he was still dripping wet with beer.

"And what have you...squirrels...brought us?" asked the Leader, Number One.

Alex answered by proudly presenting the walnut. Nicky opened it, reached inside, and pulled out Bumble's piece of paper.

"Coordinates. For a top-secret cargo drop meant for the Resistance." Alex answered. The rats were impressed. Nicky handed it to Number One, who passed it along to the others.

"Ah, very good. We are grateful to you, Pasetti Brothers. You have done well. The Rodents of Rouen, at *your* service." Number One said. The other rats nodded and then got down to work.

Alex and Nicky watched as they pulled all the Kings, Queens and Aces out of the deck, and set the rest of the deck aside. The rats then carefully peeled the paper backing off of each card, revealing something drawn on the back. Alex and Nicky couldn't tell what it was. The rats grouped the cards face down on the table, and when properly assembled, they revealed a large and very detailed map of France and the surrounding areas. Alex and Nicky were amazed. The rats read the coordinates from the piece of paper, pointed to the map, spoke quietly among themselves, and confirmed the spot where the drop was to take place.

"Les Minquiers." said Number Two. Alex and Nicky smiled.

"That's right." said Nicky.

"We do have one question though…" asked Number One.

"Yes of course, anything…" Alex answered.

"Well, why didn't you just use the window? It would have been so much easier than going through all that trouble downstairs, don't you think?" Number One pointed to an open window behind them at the back of the attic. Alex and Nicky looked at each other dumbfounded. They couldn't believe it. They looked to Edward, who meanwhile couldn't care less. He crunched happily on a few of the nuts he picked up from the tavern floor.

"Edward, stop eating…" Alex and Nicky said together, and the Rodents of Rouen laughed. Then after a moment, they all laughed.

The mission was a success.

10

Blueprints & Blue Cheese

After hours and hours of driving, the transport truck from The Cabinet War Rooms finally arrived at Station 102's main gate and pulled up to the security checkpoint. Guards approached with flashlights and a very tired Carruthers held up his ID. Bradley, the head guard on duty stooped down to take a look.

"We've been expecting you."

Carruthers yawned. He handed Bradley their security papers. Bradley gave them a quick look and handed them back.

"Which way?" asked Carruthers.

"Up there, can't miss it. Hangar One. Lit up like a Christmas tree." Bradley pointed up and to the right. "How many men do you need to help you unload?"

"That won't be necessary. We're supposed to unload and latch it up ourselves – orders from London. You understand. Our hands only."

"Understood. I'll let the Commander know you're here."

Bradley raised the gate and the truck entered the base. Carruthers backed up to the hangar entrance, cut the engine and exited the truck. It felt good to finally stretch his legs.

He stepped into the hangar and took a good long look at *Eightball Charlie*. So this was the one, he thought; the plane that was going to fly them into harm's way and back. It was hard to imagine what life was going to be like in a few short hours. Well, he *had* requested a transfer, to get out from behind his desk, see some action, and especially to get away from those two impossible lunatics back at the War Rooms. *Be careful what you wish for*, he thought.

To his surprise, a figure dressed like a mechanic stepped out from inside the plane. When he caught sight of Carruthers he walked off hurriedly in the opposite direction. It was Smiley Reilly. Smiley grabbed his tool pushcart and wheeled it across the hangar.

"Hello There! All's well then?" Carruthers called after him.

"Yep. She's one hundred percent. Checked every inch of her myself..." Smiley didn't look back. Carruthers thought it odd that he was in such a hurry and avoided eye contact, but was glad to hear the plane was in good condition.

Behind him the soldiers lifted the crate out of the back of the truck and trotted towards the plane. They pushed and pulled the heavy crate up into *Eightball Charlie*'s cargo hold with a loud CLUNK. Carruthers snapped his fingers, hustled over to the truck and pulled out the canister with a grunt.

"Can't forget you, can I?" He eased it down to the ground with a loud CLANG, then climbed back into the truck and came out with two parachute kits. The soldiers pulled the canister into the cargo hold.

"'Chutes for both then?" asked the first soldier.

"Yes indeed."

The first soldier unrolled several canvas belts to tie up the big crate, while the second soldier strapped one of the parachutes onto the top of the canister. He set the canister out of sight against the back corner of the cargo hold. Together the men then turned their full attention to the Top-Secret crate, attached the parachute and clipped the rip cord to the overhead cable, so that when the crate is pushed out of the plane, the overhead cable automatically pulls the rip cord and opens the parachute. They tested all the cables and belts and made sure everything was secure. It was. The Top-Secret Communications Device was ready to go.

Now whether it was the long drive, the lack of food or sleep, or just plain forgetfulness, once the big crate was done, the men were done, and they exited the plane. The supply canister was left leaning against the back corner, completely forgotten. The men closed the big cargo door behind them and stood guard. Their orders were to remain there until the flight crew arrived, no one in or out of the plane under any conditions until then.

A jeep approached carrying Commander Hammond. He acted like a father arriving at the hospital to see his newborn child.

"Is it here? It's here! Good show!" he called out as the jeep pulled to a stop. He jumped out and approached Carruthers.

"It's here." Carruthers replied and saluted.

"Splendid. You and your men must be starving." Hammond motioned to the jeep driver who carried over a box of food. "Not much of a selection at this time of night I'm afraid, but can you make do with a few sandwiches and some hot coffee?"

"Thank you kindly, Sir." Carruthers pulled out a sandwich and motioned to his men. He took a big grateful bite. The men standing guard approached and pulled out sandwiches of their own.

"Thank you, Sir." they said, then turned right around and headed back into the hangar.

Hammond was impressed.

"And so, my good man, you are going to navigate our flight into glory tomorrow?"

"I will do my best, Sir."

"Of course you will. Let's go, my boy. A few last-minute details we need to attend to…"

Hammond motioned Carruthers into the jeep and they sped off towards the tower. As they stood guard, Carruthers' men happily ate their sandwiches.

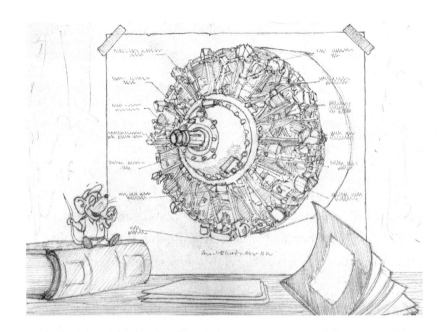

In Crash's quarters, Bumble sat on top of the cluttered desk and munched happily on his last handful of blue cheese. "Grill Sergeant" Stevens, the base's cook and Crash's buddy, had been happy to give Bumble a small sample. Even though it was only Air Force cheese, it was the first cheese Bumble had eaten in a very long time, and it was delicious. He savored every nibble and happily hummed to himself as he looked around.

Crash sat on his bed writing a letter to his family, while above him in the top bunk, his roommate Victor Wisniewski snored loudly. As Victor was officially free from navigation duty on the upcoming flight, he took the opportunity to sleep, and did so with gusto. Bumble did his best to ignore the noise by focusing on things in the room.

Above the desk was taped a large and slightly torn blueprint of the Pratt and Whitney R-1830 Twin Wasp Engine, the type used on the C-47s at the base and lots of other aircraft.

It was very impressive. From studying the blueprint, Bumble immediately understood how the engine worked, how it breathed, pumped fuel and charged electricity. The R-1830 was built like a tank, which was a good thing, as Bumble didn't want to see anything bad happen to his new friend Crash.

Also on the desk, he glanced at a pile of manuals related to the C-47s at the base, many of which he had already read. But one thing in particular caught Bumble's eye that he hadn't seen before – a War Department technical manual called "Instructions For Learning International Morse Characters". He had heard of Morse code, but didn't know much about it. He spread the manual open to the official symbol chart. It was fascinating – dots and dashes represented letters and numbers – and when they were strung together, they formed words and sentences that could be understood very easily by the trained ear or eye. Bumble studied the chart, with its letters and numbers on one side, and dots and dashes on the other.

Isn't that something... he thought to himself.

Meanwhile, in his room in the next building, Davenport lined up a putt while Chief sat on the bed and watched. Neither of them could sleep. Well, truth be told, it was Davenport who couldn't sleep, and his constant fidgeting around the room was keeping Chief awake. Not that Chief minded. He was happy his Person was excited. Once his Person was off on the mission, he could catch up on some sleep. He wanted to be rested when they got back, as there would be lots to celebrate.

Davenport looked out the window. Across the way, all lit up, was the main hangar with *Eightball Charlie* clearly visible inside. She was ready to go.

"Big day tomorrow, old buddy…"   He looked at his watch. "Today actually. Today's the day. Big day. Big day today." He swung the putter and missed the hole by a mile. "Hope I fly better than I putt." He stared out the window.

And all across Station 102, the base collectively held its breath.

Would the mission succeed?

Would *Eightball Charlie* get back safely?

Would HQ shut them down?

Only time would tell.

Takeoff

Bumble woke up to the sound of distant thunder. It was first light, and he quietly made his way outside. The early morning air was heavy with a drizzly mist, the sky was overcast, and the base was oddly quiet. *Eightball Charlie* had been moved out of the hangar and now waited patiently at the head of Runway Two. After all of the buildup, all of the meetings and all of the preparations, it was finally time. The mission was here. Bumble was excited that it was happening of course, but couldn't help but feel a little sad about not being part of Station 102's greatest hour.

HQ would probably wait to see whether the weather conditions cleared up before takeoff. Once they gave the go-ahead, things would happen very quickly. But right now, it was quiet. Bumble put his hands in his pockets as he shuffled along. It was a shame he and Chief hadn't found that missing connector ring, especially with all that was at stake today.

Bumble stared at the plane, and couldn't find any of the Tire Tread Task Force on duty – they should be here to inspect the tires before takeoff. Ed and Fred had new responsibilities now, and today of all days they should be out here making sure everything was correct. Well, it was no longer his problem, was it?

He sighed and turned towards the mess hall, not sure of what else to do.

But for every step he took, he felt an almost magnetic pull from the plane. Her tires needed checking. If he were to do it now, before anyone else came out, at least his conscience would be clear, knowing she was okay before takeoff. Despite everything, Bumble still cared, and darn it if he couldn't take just a quick peek to make sure everything looked okay. What would be the harm in that?

Bumble ran towards the plane as fast as he could. He stopped at the edge of the runway and looked up to see the two soldiers looming high above him, standing guard at the cargo door. He had to get past them without being seen. He paused and caught his breath. Thunder rumbled in the distance. What to do?

Then a sudden gust of wind blew a crumpled piece of sandwich paper from the empty food box at the soldier's feet – as it started rolling, Bumble ran alongside it as best he could. It hid him perfectly. He made it all the way to the port side wheel without being seen, then looked up at *Eightball Charlie*'s undercarriage and smiled.

Bumble climbed up on the tire, inspected the treads and immediately found multiple rocks stuck deep in the grooves. He shook his head, pulled out his shovel and started digging them out. It was a good thing he was here to do this! And, truth be told, the work felt good. Five or six rocks later, Bumble had a thought. A nagging thought that wouldn't leave him alone. Only a few feet above him was the wheel well. Up in that wheel well was supposed to be a connector ring. If it was in place, then *Eightball Charlie* was safe, but if it wasn't, then she could be in trouble. And no one knew about the missing ring on *Ace's High* except him and Chief. What harm would it be to take a peek?

He thought long and hard about what to do. Something in his gut told him to go look. He put the shovel back into his tool belt and started climbing up the landing gear.

At that very moment, Davenport, Crash and Carruthers walked out of the hangar. HQ had decided to start the mission early and to use the rainy conditions to their advantage – they thought grey skies would provide good cover for the low flying aircraft. Davenport carried a leather briefcase in one hand and several map tubes in the other. He motioned to Carruthers as they walked towards the plane.

"I'd shake your hand, but I haven't got a spare. What's your name?"

"Carruthers. Archibald Carruthers."

"Archibald?! Mind if I call you Archie?"

"Not at all. What's yours?"

"You can call me Captain."

Davenport thumped Crash in the arm with the map tubes. "Hey Crash, you got your lucky rabbit's foot, four leaf clover or whatever it is? You're going to need it today, boy."

Crash ignored the joke and extended his hand to Carruthers. "I'm Eugene, but everyone around here calls me 'Crash' so I suppose you might as well do the same."

The soldiers opened the cargo door and Davenport climbed into *Eightball Charlie* first, followed by Crash then Carruthers. All three looked at the top-secret crate. There it was. A moment of silence passed between them. Carruthers was surprised at how different it looked sitting here in the plane, more important somehow. Davenport headed up towards the cockpit while the soldiers readied to close the cargo door behind them.

"All in?" they asked.

"All in." Crash answered.

"Good luck." The door slammed shut.

Down in the wheel well, Bumble felt the bump of the door close. Above, he could hear the footsteps of the men heading up into the cockpit. He better move fast. He climbed up another few inches and tested the hydraulic hose – it looked fine – and to his relief, the connector ring was also in place. The port wheel checked out, now for the starboard. Bumble carefully climbed out of the wheel well and down the landing gear.

In the cockpit, Davenport was already strapped in as Crash took the co-pilot's seat and Carruthers sat down at the navigator's desk. Davenport flipped the first switch.

"Battery switch on."

A low hum vibrated through the cockpit as the electrical systems activated. He opened the throttle, set the engine for maximum RPM, and flipped the master ignition switch. The engine chugged and coughed. Smoke billowed out of the exhaust pipe and the propeller blades started spinning – slowly at first, then faster and faster. The port engine was now alive, and it was loud.

Crash checked the oil, fuel and hydraulic pressure – all were good. They began to do the same for the starboard engine.

Meanwhile Bumble dug all the rocks out of the starboard tire as fast as he could, but when he hurried, his work got sloppy, and the rocks weren't coming out as easily as they should have. One in particular was really jammed in there and gave him trouble. Precious seconds ticked away as he struggled with it and finally pried it loose. Just as he finished and started climbing up the landing gear, right in front of him the starboard propeller began to turn, slowly at first, then faster and faster. He hurried his climbing as thick smoke coughed out of the engine exhaust pipe. The propeller quickly spun to full speed. The vibrations in the wheel well increased as Bumble checked his grip and inched his way upward. He heard a loud rusty screech as the brakes were released. The plane began moving, and his heart started pounding in his chest. He looked down to see the ground moving below, and he could feel dizzying panic begin to creep across every inch of his body. He squeezed his eyes shut to try and calm himself. He could easily make a jump for it in just a few seconds before the plane took off, but it would be close. He reached out with a shaking hand to touch the hydraulic hose. It felt wet. He opened his eyes and saw that his hand was covered in oil. He looked up – the connector ring was missing – unscrewed from the wall, just like on *Ace's High*. It was all happening again. *Eightball Charlie* was sabotaged, and the realization made Bumble's fur stand on end.

The plane started picking up speed, and the engines increased to full throttle. They were taking off. If he were to make a jump for it, it was now or never. But the crew – his new friend Crash who gave him cheese – and the top-secret cargo – were in danger. If he jumped to safety now, they could all die and the cargo would be lost. How could he live with himself if he did nothing? He had to warn them. He had to do *something*. The noise of the engines became deafening, and the vibrations shook him until he almost lost his grip. A ferocious wind started blowing inside the wheel well and it took all of his strength just to hold on. The runway started flashing by below him, faster and faster. Dizziness washed over him in waves and he closed his eyes again. His breathing became frantic and his heart now felt like it was going to burst out of his chest. Just don't look down. Don't look down.

In spite of his terror, Bumble knew what he had to do.

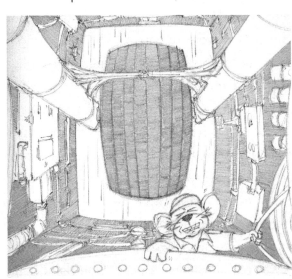 Too much of his life was spent in regret of actions not taken, paths not followed and giving up on things too easily. Well no more. Right now, this very moment, what's right is right, and to jump off the plane and save his own skin when he knew others could die was something he simply could not do.

The nose of the plane began to rise, and within moments the runway shrank away beneath them. The landing gear automatically lifted up into the wheel wells, settling into locked position below Bumble. *Eightball Charlie* was airborne, and Bumble Humblestone was with them.

12

The Spinning Wheel
Of Doom

The English countryside whizzed by below. Cottages, farms, tractors and cows all looked like pieces of a children's board game. A very fast-moving board game. Bumble marveled at the sight between tiny trembling fingers cupped over his eyes. The reality of his situation had now settled in. How in his right mind could he have actually decided to stay on board? Was he nuts, or was he simply stupid? Maybe a little of both. Or maybe this was something new? Maybe he was brave. He lowered his hand to see everything around him.

Bumble wondered how many mice had ever seen the world like this, from high up in the air. Considering the mice he knew, it couldn't have been many, so on the positive side, he could be the first. On the not so positive side, he might also be the last if he wasn't careful. He wasn't going to last much longer hiding in the wheel well – either he would grow tired and lose his grip, or the wind and vibrations would shake him loose. Plus, the wet and slippery conditions weren't helping either. He had to get inside the plane.

From his position, he could see that across the other side of the wheel well there was a small gap between the junction box and the gear sprockets – a space just big enough for him to fit – which would take him inside the wing and out of immediate danger. To get to it, he would have to get across the enormous starboard tire – second nature to him – as long as he didn't look down of course. But what Bumble didn't know, was that engine vibrations in the wheel well often caused tires to rotate on their own, sometimes very quickly.

"Up you go!" he said to himself.

He grabbed hold of a small switch box and pulled himself up to a jumping position. He coiled like a spring against the back wall, then thrust himself into the air and onto the tire, hitting the hard rubber.

"Oof!"

He waited a moment, caught his breath, and then started to climb. The tire was still wet from the runway, but Bumble gripped the treads like the expert he was – and in no time he was at the top of the wheel. The gap was right in front of him, one small jump away.

And that's when the tire started to turn.

It turned slowly at first, and Bumble took a step forward to correct his position. But as the wheel continued to move, he had to take another step, and another, and quicker and faster and before he knew it he was running on the spinning wheel like a crazed hamster, trying to stay in place. This was some pickle he was now in.

"FIIIIIBLEJIIIIIIBIIIIITS!" he yelled.

The rubber was slippery and the wheel was turning fast and he was going to fly right out of the plane unless he thought of something this very instant. His heart stuck in his throat as he did the only thing he could think of – he dropped flat, laid face down on the tire and held onto the treads for dear life.

If Bumble had been frightened during takeoff, the experience of circling around and around on the starboard wheel was worse. A lot worse. The wheel spun and spun, and he was swept out under the plane, then back into the wheel well, then back out, then back in again.

"WAAAAHHHHH!!!!!" he screamed, and squeezed his eyes shut.

Over and over and over he whirled. He was getting dizzy and would surely fly away if it didn't slow down – which, after what seemed like forever, it finally did. The tire came to a rest and Bumble found himself back at the top of the wheel, in the wheel well, right where he had started.

He peeked one eye open to make sure he wasn't still moving. He wasn't, but he sure felt like he was. He not only had a spell of dizziness, he had a fit, an attack, an assault, a *bombardment* of dizziness. He opened the other eye and the inside of the wheel well spun and whirled around like a ship on the high seas. All Bumble could do was lie there and catch his breath and try to settle down. What a pickle, he thought, and the thought made him sick.

Then, after only a minute or so of resting, the wheel budged. It was going to start turning again. Bumble swallowed hard and gathered all of the strength he could to get up and get moving. He staggered up to his feet as everything continued to pinwheel around him. His hands were clenched and stiff from holding on to the tire. He could feel the wheel inch forward and then roll back, threatening to break out into a full spin. There wasn't much time. Bumble got his bearings and looked for the gap he had seen earlier. In his blurred vision, the gap swayed from left to right, then right to left. Bumble decided to make the jump when the gap was in the middle, more or less. He blinked hard and took a deep breath. And then he jumped.

Bumble flew through the air, right on target. But what he couldn't see, thanks to his dizziness, was a sharp tiny metal screw sticking out close to the gap. A bolt must have worked itself loose over the years exposing the screw head, and it was pointed straight at him. He landed and clipped the tip of his right ear on the screw. He saw stars.

"YEEOOOW!"

Despite the pain, Bumble grabbed onto a nearby hose and got his footing. Below him, the wheel had again started to turn, and below that, endless open space. He was very grateful to have made it. He crawled inside the gap, into the darkness of the wing interior, and collapsed.

13

Course: One-Eight-Nine

In the cockpit, all was quiet except for the roar of the engines. The men were all focused on starting their mission tasks. Crash's mouth had gone dry and he had trouble swallowing. Carruthers tapped his fingers on the empty map table in front of him in the navigator's station. Both of them were very nervous. Davenport tried to lighten the mood.

"Almost time. Once we're over open water I'm allowed to give you your orders. In the meantime..." Davenport checked the contents of his leather briefcase and pulled out a shiny silver revolver. He set it on the glare panel above the instruments.

"This...is reserved for new navigators who get us lost on their first flight."

He was kidding of course, and Carruthers pulled out his own pistol and set it on the map table, much to Davenport's surprise.

"Well, I'll know we're lost long before you do, Sir..." he replied.

Crash grinned. "I think he got you."

"Yes, I think you're right." Davenport admitted with a smile. He reached out his hand. "I'll take that. You'll get it back if we have to land on a deserted island somewhere and get attacked by dinosaurs or zombies..." Carruthers reluctantly offered up the pistol.

"What about Germans?" Carruthers asked.

"Yep, especially those. Holler if you see any."

Davenport put both pistols in his briefcase and latched it closed.

Inside the wing, the space vibrated violently, and the starboard engine made a tremendous noise. Bumble sat up and got his bearings. It was almost pitch black and it took his eyes some time to adjust. He sniffed the air and could smell fumes coming from a nearby gas tank, and although his right ear ached and throbbed terribly, he could clearly hear fuel sloshing around the inside of the tank. Even though the space was dark, cramped and smelly, it was still better than spinning around on that horrible wheel of doom.

As his eyes adjusted, a beam of light became visible in the murky darkness. There was a small hole – an opening meant for an emergency fuel hose – and it looked like he would fit. Bumble needed to get into the cockpit and warn Crash about the missing connector ring, so he stood up, swayed a little, and walked on wobbly legs towards the hole. He could hear Davenport's muffled voice on the other side. He eased his head into the hole, winced as his ear rubbed against the metal, and popped out under the radio operator's station behind the co-pilot.

Davenport was in the middle of saying "...and that starboard engine is about as unstable as my first wife. So pay close attention. I'm serious. If you sneeze the engine might lose pump pressure and start leaking again. One other thing – to get her ready in time, the maintenance team had to make one major sacrifice – the autopilot is off and can't be used. One of us has got to be up here on the stick at all times." He looked out the window as they cleared the English coast and were now over open water. "Okay gents it's official – time for us to hit the deck." He pushed the wheel forward and pitched *Eightball Charlie* down close to the water and under radar range. At full throttle, they should reach their target in a very short time. The mission had begun.

"Course one-eight-nine degrees," he continued, which meant a heading almost due south and just a little west. But Bumble already knew they were headed south to the Channel Islands. Davenport passed a map tube back to Carruthers, who popped the cap and spread the map over his desk. Bumble's eyes went wide at the site of the map, as the memory of his inky footprint misadventure came flooding back. He watched the new guy to see how he would react to seeing the footprints, but even after a few moments, there was no reaction. Bumble guessed that he was being professional and ignoring them.

"Now that we're over water, here are the orders – our mission packets." Davenport reached into his briefcase, and Bumble gulped as the captain pulled the envelopes out. Now his footprints would be revealed for all to see. No missing them this time. The ruined Top-Secret mission packets, ruined by one Bumble Humblestone, the clumsy, stumbling, fumbling mouse who stepped in black ink and – wait a minute – Bumble squinted to make sure he was seeing this right. The mission packets were different – they were clean. These were new envelopes. No footprints or big red "X"s anywhere to be seen. Headquarters must have sent new ones after the mess he made. This was good news. Crash and Carruthers opened their envelopes and started reading. Bumble smiled in relief as Davenport continued the briefing.

"Our objective is the Channel Island of Jersey. We are to maintain strict radio silence all the way to the target and back. The drop will be inland, over the capital, Saint Helier near the southern coast. Once we've made the drop, I mean the *instant* it's out of the plane, we turn tail, get the heck outta there and fly straight back up to base no questions asked." The men nodded, but Bumble's relieved smile sank into a concerned frown.

This was not what he had seen for himself the day before. Not at all. They were supposed to make their way *around* Jersey, down to the Minkies and make the drop there, not drop it *on* Jersey. Jersey was occupied. The Minkies were uninhabited. The whole point of dropping it on the Minkies was to make it available for the Resistance to pick up later, and to prevent the Germans from getting it.

Davenport continued, "There's a pocket of Resistance fighters on Jersey who know we're coming and will be looking for us – and they'll grab the crate before the Germans do. We've just got to drop it on the right spot at the right time and they'll take it from there." Crash and Carruthers nodded yes, but Bumble shook his head no. Why would headquarters change the drop site from yesterday? He had seen the original map himself, the drop site was very clear. Something was fishy. Too much was already going wrong here – first the sabotage in the wheel well, now the misdirected mission orders. Maybe the new guy wasn't being polite – maybe the map had been switched along with the mission packets. Bumble decided he would have to take a look at the map himself, and based on what he saw, he would figure out what to do. No one knew he was aboard, and he should try to use that to his advantage and keep hidden for as long as possible. Time to do a little sneaking around.

Meanwhile, back at Station 102, Chief woke up with a loud snort. He had overslept and felt very groggy. He stood up on Davenport's bed and shook his head to try to clear the cotton from between his ears. Then he had a nice long stretch and a big yawn. Outside the window he could see that it was raining. *Oh well, time to get wet...* he thought. He was hungry and had to do his business. Still groggy, he stepped to the foot of the bed, slipped on Davenport's footlocker and tumbled to the floor with a loud thud. He kicked his legs to get upright and knocked his Person's shoes clear across the room. He heard multiple metallic TINK-TINK-TINKS. Then he froze. His fur stood on end. In front of him, on the floor, were two hydraulic hose connector rings.

It took him a minute to realize what he was looking at. They had tumbled out of his Person's shoes. The notorious connector rings – "We find those, we find the saboteur…" is what Bumble had said. The realization of what he was seeing started to sink in. How could his Person be the saboteur? It was unthinkable. He was a hero, the best pilot at the base. But there was the terrible proof! Chief stared at the connector rings and felt a knot in his stomach.

Even worse, there were two of them. The first one would have been from *Ace's High,* that much was obvious, but it was the second one that concerned him. Which of the planes did it come from? The knot in his stomach tightened as he realized it could only be one plane: *Eightball Charlie.* Of course it was. The mission was in jeopardy.

Chief barked the loudest bark he had ever barked. He pushed at the door with his nose. It didn't budge. In all the time they lived there Davenport never locked the door – except for yesterday and today. Chief barked again and again. No one heard him. He jumped back up on the bed and barked at the closed window. There were men working in the distance, but because it was raining no one saw him. He jumped back down and scratched at the door again. He was trapped and wondered what he could do.

"Squirrel-snippets! Thimble-jinkets!" What was it that Bumble always said when he was upset? Oh well, it didn't matter.

Out of the corner of his eye, in the corner of the room, he saw the hole in the floor that his Person, no – the saboteur – had used for putting practice. He scrambled over to the hole and called out "Bumble! Bumble can you hear me? I'm locked in here! Help!"

Chief was greatly concerned. He was concerned for the mission. He was concerned that his Person was not who he had appeared to be. And he was concerned that he had to do his business and the door was locked.

Now it just so happened that Mortimer the mole was tunneling nearby and heard Chief's call for help from under the floorboards. He popped up in a sea of golf balls. "Hello? Is someone in need of assistance? Goodness Gracious, what's with all of these projectiles?"

"Hey, Mr. Mole!" Chief struggled to remember the mole's name. Boy, he really was groggy. What was it? Monty? Malcolm? Mortimer! "Mortimer the Mole! Can you hear me?"

"Yes, I can. What we moles lack in sight we make up for in hearing, so there is no need to shout."

"I'm sorry. It's just that I've been locked in, trapped."

"Trapped? A prisoner you say? This is most peculiar, most irregular what's going on around here if you ask me..."

"I couldn't agree with you more. So – please – can you find someone to unlock this door? Today's big mission is in jeopardy."

Mortimer was shocked, then enraged, and moved with purpose. "Mission? Jeopardy? I'll not stand for that! I'm on my way, and will have your door open in a jiff!"

"Bite them if you have to! Just get someone to open this door!" Chief exclaimed. With that, Mortimer tore under the barracks to find his volunteer.

Victor Wisniewski exited his sleeping barracks and shuffled along the path towards the mess hall. He was in a good mood despite the rain, thanks to the opportunity to sleep in. As he rounded the corner of the next building, he came face to face with Mortimer, who blocked the path and made loud chattering noises as if he was trying to communicate. In fact he was, but humans can't understand mole, so Mortimer's efforts were in vain.

Wisniewski looked down at the noisy little creature and found him to be adorable in an ugly kind of way. He attempted to sidestep around Mortimer to the right, but the mole moved to the right and blocked him. He tried to sidestep to the left, but Mortimer followed, stood his ground and kept chattering. He seemed very passionate about something.

"You're a strange little bugger," he said. "Why are you bothering me, then?"

Mortimer scurried over to the barracks door and back, chattering loudly. He waved his little mole arms. "Listen here you! Open this door – the mission could be lost and it'll be YOUR fault! Do you hear me? Lost! Because of YOU! Seconds count! Open this door this very instant!" He bared his teeth and pointed his little mole arm at Wisniewski and made a loud determined squeak. He was ready to bite if need be. Maybe it was a good thing humans didn't understand mole. But the strategy worked. In-between all the chattering, Wisniewski had stood long enough in front of Davenport's door to hear Chief scratching at it from the inside.

"Hold on," he said and crossed over and listened at the door. Chief sniffed him through the bottom of the doorframe and started barking. "Hey Chief, is that you in there boy?" Mortimer shook his head as if to ask, "Who else would it be?" and Wisniewski tried the handle. No luck. Chief's barking turned to yelps and whines, and grew louder and more desperate. He sounded like he was in trouble. Wisniewski looked around to see if anyone was nearby to help. As far as he knew Davenport had the only key. Maybe there was a master key somewhere in Hammond's office, but the dog sounded like he really had to get out, so Wisniewski threw his shoulder into the door and it popped open easily.

Chief burst out into the rain. Time to do his business. Wisniewski smiled and started to walk on. No – wait! Chief held it in and ran at Wisniewski. He pulled at Wisniewski's pant leg and ran back into the barracks. Wisniewski looked down at the mole who was still "eyeing" him with hostility, looking for a fight. This was certainly strange. Chief barked loudly from inside.

Wisniewski walked into Davenport's quarters and looked at Chief. "What boy?" Chief circled the middle of the room, then pawed at the floor, and Wisniewski finally saw what

Chief wanted him to see. The connector rings. Wisniewski's eyes went wide with recognition. He shook his head, blinked a few times as the full implications of what he saw sunk in.

"Holy moley! HOLY MOLEY!"

Mortimer shook his head and grumbled to himself. "Why do people insist on saying that? You don't hear me saying 'Holy Human' or some such thing! It's small-minded, that's what it is."

Wisniewski grabbed the rings off the floor and bolted out into the rain. Chief followed him out and stood next to Mortimer, and they watched Wisniewski run as fast as he could to the control tower in the distance.

"Now we're getting somewhere," said Mortimer. "Feels good to make a difference, doesn't it?"

"Yep, feels good," Chief answered as he lifted his leg and finally did his business. "Really good."

Wisniewski burst into the control tower. Hammond was going through a stack of shipment orders at his desk while a private swept the floor. They both looked up in surprise.

"That thing on?" Wisniewski said and pointed to the main communications radio. The private barely had a chance to reply "Yes…" as Wisniewski dropped the connector rings on top of Hammond's paperwork, then sat down at the radio and put on the headset. The files in Hammond's hand dropped to the floor as he looked at the rings in front of him. He knew exactly what they were and what they meant. Wisniewski started frantically turning dials. "It's Davenport…" he said and found the correct radio frequency. Hammond got up and stood next to Wisniewski as Victor spoke into the microphone.

"*Eightball Charlie*, this is Station 102, do you read me? Come in – over?"

Hammond put on a pair of headphones and grabbed the microphone for himself.

"*Eightball Charlie*…do you read me?!" Hammond said.

"*EIGHTBALL CHARLIE…DO YOU READ ME?*" he repeated with urgency.

Together, they listened for a reply, but there was nothing.

Nothing but static…and then…silence.

14

Over And Out

*E*ightball *Charlie* raced south, skimming the water. The engines were holding speed and there were no enemy planes in sight. Only a few fishing boats drifted by below, and a handful of angry French fisherman shook their fists at the plane's high speed, loud noise and low altitude. One of them raised an old rifle and fired off a blind shot at the noisy plane just for spite. The bullet lodged itself somewhere inside the port engine. Nothing happened though, and *Eightball Charlie* continued speeding on her way.

Through the windshield, out on the horizon, the outline of Jersey Island was fast approaching. "Target ahead," said Davenport as he got up out of his seat. "We only get one shot at this." He pointed to Crash. "You take the wheel. I'm going to open the hatch and check the crate one last time." He pointed to Carruthers. "Give me a hand, would you Archie?"

They exited the cockpit and Davenport closed the compartment door behind them.

Bumble sprang into action. From his hiding place under the radio console, he ran to the navigator's station, climbed up the leg of the table and scrambled across the flight map to see for himself just what the heck was going on. He followed the flight path, and saw that what was once a low arching loop around the bottom of Jersey had now become a straight line leading directly to the center of the island. And, to his previous relief but now growing alarm, none of his inky footprints were anywhere to be seen.

It was just as he had feared. The map had been switched, and the orders had been changed. It *was* sabotage, and the unthinkable was happening right before his eyes. They were about to drop the top-secret crate over enemy territory. Every molecule in his body ignited with intensity. He had to do something. Anything. And so he decided to do the one thing a mouse was never supposed to do. He would talk.

He called out to his friend Crash, but over the roar of the engines and all of the noise booming around in the cockpit, Bumble's little voice was lost. Besides, Crash was so wrapped up in holding *Eightball Charlie* on course, it was doubtful he would have heard anything anyway. He would have to get into Crash's field of vision. The island was getting closer.

Bumble jumped from the navigator's table to the pilot's chair, then onto the control pedestal. He stepped carefully around the control levers. The last thing he wanted to do was touch something and add to the already dangerous situation.

He yelled up to Crash, "HELLO!" and waved his hand, but no response. He started climbing up the instrument panel. From one dial to the next he climbed like an expert rock-climber. The vibrations in the cockpit shook the panel terribly and he almost lost his grip, but  he managed to make it all the way to the top and stood on the glare panel right under Crash's line of sight. Out the window, Bumble could see the island was very close. He waved his arms and yelled as loud as he could.

"HEY! HAAAAAY! Down heeeeere!"

Crash blinked as his concentration was finally broken. He couldn't believe his eyes and ears.

"AAHH! Hey! Little Buddy! Wait - you can talk?!"

"Long story I'm afraid!" Bumble answered.

"What in the world are you doing here??"

"We're in trouble!" Bumble screamed back and continued, "The plane is sabotaged. The hydraulic hose connector ring has been removed! And we're going the wrong way! These orders have been faked..."

Crash couldn't believe what Bumble was saying. "It's true! Yesterday I saw the originals for myself..." He pointed to the map on the navigator's station. "This map is different. These orders are different. We're supposed to drop the crate *south* of the island, not *on* the island. No one's waiting to pick it up - except the enemy!" It took a second for the information to sink in. "My name is Bumble, by the way..." Bumble tipped his cap and offered his hand for a shake.

Just then, Davenport re-entered the cockpit. Bumble jumped down into Crash's front pocket as Davenport took his seat and looked out the window intently. The island was just within reach now. Davenport cleared his throat and grabbed the controls tightly.

"Looking good. Time to break radar cover and take her up to 1,000 feet – that should be just enough distance for the parachute to open and touch this box down safely, so get ready..." He and Crash exchanged a quick glance, and then Davenport called out "...NOW!"

They both pulled back on their control wheels and *Eightball Charlie* shot up into the sky. Below them the marshy beachfront of the north end of Jersey started to shrink away. They were now over the island. Davenport pushed the engines hard as they climbed. It was a moment of eerie calm as their view was filled with sky before they leveled off.

"Answer me this, Eugene. You volunteered, right? Why did you sign up?" Davenport asked. Davenport never called Crash "Eugene". Something was happening. "Was this what you signed up for? To be a delivery man? I doubt it. It can't be! Last week, I go grab a drink at that crappy bar the next town over. Fighter pilots everywhere. They see the ATC badge on my hat – do you know what they call us at Station 102? Not Air Transport Command, I can tell you that. They call us the 'Airline Of Terrified Civilians'. Can you believe it? No respect." Davenport paused for effect. The altimeter read 400 feet.

Davenport poked his thumb into his chest. "We're pilots – pilots just like them. With all of what's going on in the war, they've got us flying *cargo*? We're the best pilots at the base Eugene, and what's it get us? Nothing. I should be a Colonel by now, but I've been passed over. You have too – you just don't know it yet."

Crash looked down at Bumble, who pointed at Davenport, then gave a little "thumbs down" and held his nose as if something smelled. The plane continued to rise.

"I don't know about you, but I joined up to fly bombers, not pilot flying trucks."

The altimeter read 800 feet.

"I want to drop bombs, not cans of mystery meat, drums of gasoline or boxes of matches." He pointed out of the window and stabbed at the sky with his index finger. "There will be thousands of bombers in the sky this time next year, and they've only got us flying cargo?! Think about it."

The altimeter read 1,000 feet. Davenport pushed the control wheel forward and Crash followed his lead. *Eightball Charlie* leveled out. They were about a quarter of the way over the island. Davenport stared straight ahead, lost in his thoughts.

"Well, not me. I'll fly for whoever will give me the chance to do something important. Germany is on the hunt for

American pilots with special skills, and now that they've found me, I'm not about to keep them waiting. It's been in the works for a while."

Crash couldn't believe what he was hearing. Too much was happening all at once. Bumble was right. The mission *was* falling apart. Davenport reached up, put his thumb on the Starboard Propeller Feathering Button and turned to Crash one last time.

"This is it. I'm sorry old buddy, but you're about to lose one engine. Remember everything I taught you and you might make it home alive. Time for me to go. Good luck. I really hope you make it."

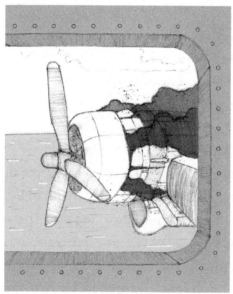

And with that, he pushed the button and left the cockpit. After a moment, the starboard engine started to sputter, shake, and groan to a halt. The propeller stopped turning and the cockpit shook violently as thick black smoke started pouring out of the engine. Crash looked at it in disbelief.

In the cargo hold, Davenport checked the unconscious body of Archie Carruthers, whom he had surprised with a blinding uppercut that had knocked him out cold when they went to 'check the crate'. He pulled out a pair of handcuffs and shackled Carruthers' left hand to the wall by the first starboard window.

Davenport then hustled to the back of the plane and opened the cargo doors. Wind whipped inside the cargo hold as he checked one last time that the parachute ripcord was properly attached to the crate, and then, with all of his might, he pushed the Top-Secret Communications Device through the open door and out of the plane. The ripcord pulled just like it should, and the crate floated away into open space. Davenport then checked the buckles on his own parachute, and jumped out of *Eightball Charlie*. His parachute opened and he drifted away in the same direction as the crate, down into occupied territory.

Back in the cockpit, Bumble climbed out of Crash's pocket, and Crash placed him back up on the glare panel. "What are we going to do?" Crash yelled. He turned around and looked towards the back of the plane. "It's gone! The crate's gone! The Captain's gone! I can't believe it!" Crash was beside himself. His eyes were practically popping out of his head. "Where's the new guy? Did he get thrown out too??" Wind from the open door blew everything around the inside of the plane. Loose papers flew everywhere in the cockpit.

"I'll go look!" Bumble said.

He jumped down from the glare panel to the empty Captain's chair and ran out of the cockpit as fast as he could. In the cargo hold he immediately found Carruthers handcuffed and unconscious. Bumble ran up his arm and started yelling in his ear.

"Hey Corporal! Corporal Whoever-You-Are! Wakey wakey! Wake up! Waaaaake uuuuuuup!" Bumble smacked his cheek, pinched his nose and pulled his earlobe. No use, the guy was out cold.

Bumble ran back down his arm.   He was about to turn towards the cockpit when out of the corner of his eye he saw it – sitting in the back of the cargo hold, all by itself – the canister! Davenport had left it behind. Bumble snapped his fingers and ran back up to the cockpit with a big grin on his face.

"The mission's not over!" Bumble shouted as he climbed back up on the Captain's chair.

Just then, the cockpit shook as the starboard engine finally died.

"Yes it is!" Crash hollered. Bumble was determined.

"It can't be! The canister is *still on board*. We can still do this!" Bumble pointed to the cargo hold. "It's not over!"

Crash pointed out the window at the dead engine. "If we don't get that engine working, we're done for – Lord knows if we can make it all the way home on just one. The cargo is gone. And we're going down. I'm sorry little buddy, but the mission is over, and we lost." Crash started to turn the control wheel to head back home.

"Wait!" Bumble shrieked. He swallowed hard, stood up straight and looked Crash square in the eye. "What if I could fix it? Fix the engine. If I can get it going again, would you finish the job and drop the canister? At least drop this one where it's supposed to be dropped? Over the Minkies…"

"The what?" Crash asked.

"The Minkies. That's what I was trying to tell you. We were supposed to drop everything over a formation of uninhabited rocks nine miles south of the island – they're straight ahead, we can't miss them!"

Crash looked at the instruments, made a few mental calculations and nodded. "Alright, yes. I can keep us steady for a few more minutes. What are you going to do?"

"Remember that engine blueprint in your room? The one you never look at? I got a good look at it last night and think the long-range fuel shut-off valve is wonky. All I have to do is climb back into the wing and mess around a bit and we should be back in business."

Bumble put on a good show, but the thought of going back into the wing frightened him. He would have to get across that horrible wheel well again. "Besides, I'm the only one around here big enough to do it. I mean small. You're the Captain now – you've got to man the controls, and Corporal What's-His-Name back there is unconscious." Crash nodded in relief, "At least he's still alive." He was moved by Bumble's determination and bravery. If this little mouse was so brave, then he should be too. "Alright. You're going in. But you've got to protect that ear of yours…" he said.

Bumble reached up, felt his ear – and winced. Yes, come to think of it, it still hurt like crazy. He looked around. Clipped to the side of the pilot's chair was a water canteen, with a cap that looked to be the right size for his tiny head. He removed the cap and carefully placed it on his head, tucked his ears in, and fastened the chain under his chin. He was fully helmeted and ready to go. Crash was impressed. He pointed at Bumble.

"You are the maintenance engineer now Bumble. You know what's wrong – you know how to fix it. Only you can save *Eightball*

Charlie – and us. It's up to you! You can do it!" Bumble stood up straight, gave a big thumbs up and answered, "I will Captain! Back in a minute!" He jumped down, and ran out of sight.

Crash looked out the side window to see the southern coast of Jersey island approaching below, and in the distance, open sea after that. He hoped Bumble knew what he was talking about and that they could reach the Minkies before more disaster struck. He pushed forward on the control wheel and brought *Eightball Charlie* back down to a low altitude, out of radar range. Even on one engine she picked up tremendous speed, and it took all of Crash's skills to keep her level and in control.

"*Flying trucks…*" he said, as his eyes locked in on the horizon.

Do It Afraid

So much had happened so quickly, that Bumble hadn't had a chance to consider how afraid he really was. Everything rested on his ability to restart this engine. As he got to the dark little hole, the seriousness of his responsibility started sinking in. But Bumble knew that if he stopped and thought about it, he would likely stop for good, so he decided he was just going to have to *do it afraid*, and eased his helmet into the hole and entered the wing for a second time.

"In you go," he said to himself.

It was dark and eerily quiet inside. Without the engine working, the wing seemed hollow and empty. The good news was, there were fewer vibrations, which would make the work easier to accomplish. The bad news was, he had to contend with the dreaded wheel well once again. He crawled through two small compartments and found the gap with the sharp screw he used for entry the first time around. His ear hurt just looking at it.

Bumble entered the wheel well compartment, and there waiting for him, was the big spinning wheel. "Ugh. Not you again," Bumble said.

This time, he took a good long look around before deciding what to do. Several thick groups of electrical wires snaked around all four walls and were tied together in such a way that they could act as a walkway around the entire space. This was good. He stepped down carefully onto the wires and started to inch his way along the wall.

To keep from looking down, he gave his full attention to all of the many tiny details in front of him – bolts, clips, worn paint – and then he saw something interesting. A faint handwritten inscription that read: "Mary B, Douglas Aircraft Company, Santa Monica Plant, June 1940." Like everyone, Bumble had heard the popular stories of "Rosie The Riveter" and the other women who had helped build the planes in America that got sent overseas to fight in Europe, but he thought they were just stories. Well, here was proof that they were true. If Mary from Santa Monica helped build *Eightball Charlie*, then he could help fix her.

In no time, Bumble got to the front side of the wheel well and crawled up into the engine compartment. The engine looked just like the blueprint: big and solid. Built like a tank. "No time to waste then..." he said to no one in particular.

Based on his memory of the blueprint, Bumble needed to find a small electrical pump towards the top of the engine that controlled the flow of oil in and out of the pistons – if he could restart it, the shut-off valves would reopen and the engine would work again. The only problem was, electricity and oil were a dangerous combination, and one small spark in the wrong place could blow everything up. One fried mouse, one crashed airplane. Best not to think of that. He had come too far today to get fried to a crisp.

He started climbing up the complex web of deflectors, pipes, nuts and lugs. He had to move fast, as every piece of metal he touched was hot. His hands were starting to feel burned. Traces of smoke also wisped around inside the compartment causing his eyes to sting and tear. He coughed and his throat felt thick. There was a lot of soot everywhere from the smoke, and Bumble got very dirty as he made his way up.

At the top of the engine, to his great relief, he found what he was looking for: the electric fuel pump. It was right where it was supposed to be according to the blueprint. He wiped the top of it clean and saw immediately what was wrong: the spark plug leads had gotten disconnected in all of the shaking the engine did when Davenport shut it down. He checked the other wires and they all seemed fine. The fuel lines were all still connected too. This should be an easy fix. Once the spark plug connector was reconnected they should be back in business.

Bumble reached down and started pulling up the loose, dangling connector. As he did, it barely touched the side of the engine's metal plating, and sparked. Bumble's fur stood on end as electric current passed through his body. ZZZZZZZZAAAAAAAAP! He dropped the connector. On second thought, this wasn't going to be such an easy fix. He would have to ease it up, ever so gently, and make sure the end did not touch anything metallic.

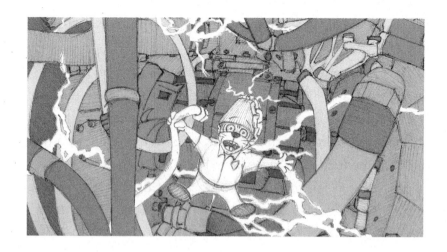

He took a deep breath, held it, and started pulling the connector up again. The end swayed slightly and he froze. The motion stopped. He pulled it up a little more at a time – stopping, waiting and pulling – until the end finally made it up into the clear. No more shocks, thank goodness. Bumble let out his breath and held the connector with trembling hands. This had been an exhausting day so far, and he was getting tired and sloppy.

He got a good grip on the connector, placed it ever-so-gently on top of the spark plug, then pushed down with all of his strength. It snapped into place. Success! It was reconnected. The fuel pump started to hum. All that needed to happen now was for Crash to hit the restart button. Bumble smiled, and hurried back to the cockpit.

Meanwhile, in the cargo hold, Carruthers started to wake up. He blinked his eyes, shook his head and got his bearings. He saw that he was handcuffed. He saw that the cargo door was open. And he saw that the crate was gone. "Blast!" he said. He rubbed his chin and grimaced.

The last thing he remembered was entering the compartment with Davenport and getting punched. "Bugger! I can't believe this!" he said. He pulled himself over as close to the cockpit door as he could.

"Eugene!" he yelled. He thumped on the metal wall with his fist. "Hey! Hello up there!" He waved his free hand in the doorway.

In the cockpit, Crash turned around to see Carruthers' waving hand. "Oh thank God!" he said and yelled "Archie! You're okay! What happened?!"

"Your *boss* is what happened – he got away with our box – and he handcuffed me back here before he bailed."

"I know! It gets worse! We're out an engine and I don't think we can make it back unless Bumble gets it fixed."

"Unless *who* does *what*??" answered Carruthers.

"Bumble!" Crash yelled.

"What's a Bumble?"

"Me!" said a tiny voice.

Carruthers looked down and saw the little mouse mechanic, covered with soot, wearing the canteen cap for a helmet. His eyes and teeth shone bright white against the dark soot.

"Blimey! A talking mouse! I must still be unconscious!" he said. Bumble smiled up at him and pointed at his shackled wrist. "Wait right there, I'll get you out of those handcuffs in just a minute..." Bumble ran off towards the cockpit.

"Yes, I'll wait right here," Carruthers answered sarcastically. As if he could do anything else.

Bumble climbed up on the captain's chair and yelled to Crash. "Everything is reconnected – the engine should work – give her a try!"

Crash reached up and put his thumb on the starter. "Here goes nothing..." he said and pushed it. The engine sputtered to life. The propeller started to turn, slowly at first, then quickly to full speed. Victory! Crash sunk back in his chair in relief.

"Well done Bumble."

"Thanks, Captain."

"Aces mouse!" yelled Carruthers. "Now help me out of these handcuffs, please!"

"Right!" Bumble jumped down and ran back to the cargo hold. Crash kept the course steady as they were now over open water.

"Hello again," Bumble said as he climbed up Carruthers' arm, leaving little soot footprints as he went.

"Hi." Archie was upset. He had been hand-picked to safeguard the top-secret cargo and had failed. Miserably. He thought of the team back at the Cabinet War Rooms, and of that enormous, complicated and beautiful communications device that took the Agents so many hours to finish. He also wondered how the Resistance would cope with the loss of the device they had been expecting and so desperately needed. It was a very bad state of affairs for him all the way around. He sighed.

"Excuse me," Bumble whispered as he snaked around the back of Archie's shoulders, up his other arm, and to his handcuffed wrist. Bumble studied the handcuffs closely and rubbed his chin in thought. He reached inside the lock compartment and felt around. It was impossible to budge.

"What do you think?" Archie asked.

"Tough one."

Bumble looked inside. He would need a key of some sort, and Davenport had obviously taken it with him when he jumped. Bumble pulled out his trusty shovel and started to work on picking the lock.

Up front, Crash could begin to see scattered rock formations, and they were approaching fast.

"Minkies, dead ahead!" he yelled.

"Oh!" Bumble stopped in his tracks. "We've got to get the canister ready."

Bumble jiggled the shovel, moved it around as hard as he could, but couldn't budge the lock. "Here, you try!" he said to Archie and hopped down. Carruthers pinched the tiny tool between his fingers and started fidgeting. It was harder than it looked.

For what seemed like the thousandth time, Bumble ran to the cockpit and climbed up the Captain's chair. Crash pointed out the window.

"There they are, just like you said. Coming up fast. Is he free yet?"

"Um, not quite."

"What do you mean 'not quite'?! He's got to push the canister out of the plane. How are we going to drop it? *I* can't do it – I have to fly the plane – and we've got no autopilot, thanks to you-know-who! Ugh! I can't believe it. What are we going to do?!"

Carruthers thumped his hand against the compartment wall.

"Turn Turtle!" he yelled.

"'*Turn Turtle*'? What does that mean?" answered Crash.

Carruthers stuck his free hand in the doorway and mimicked the shape of a plane.

"Tip the plane 'arse over elbow, like this!" He tipped his hand to the side. "Out falls the canister!" Crash turned around to see his hand signal and nodded.

"Tip the plane! Yes, *that* I understand – let's do it!" He looked down to Bumble. "Bumble, go check the canister. Make sure everything is hooked up, then we'll tip it the heck out of here and go home."

"Right!" Bumble winked a confident wink, jumped down and ran out of the cockpit for what seemed like the *two* thousandth time. He passed Carruthers.

"Still stuck?"

"Don't be funny."

"Sorry…"

Carruthers continued to fiddle with the handcuffs while Bumble ran to the canister. He climbed up on top, scrambled across the parachute, and saw that the rip cord was not hooked up to anything. It dangled limply and ended in a metal clasp that lay on the floor. He'd have to hook it up to something, or the parachute wouldn't open. He looked around quickly and saw something that would do the trick – a tie down ring bolted to the floor panel near the open door.

He slid down the cord, picked up the clasp and dragged it behind him. With great effort, he pried it open, and clipped it to the tie down ring. The clasp snapped closed. Bumble gave the thumbs up signal to Carruthers, who at that very second managed to get the handcuffs open.

"GOT IT!" Carruthers yelled excitedly.

"Drop it?" answered Crash. "Okay, here goes nothing!"

"No! No…" Carruthers started to answer, but it was too late. Crash turned the control wheel and *Eightball Charlie* pitched hard to the left. The engines groaned loudly, and everything inside the cargo hold started moving. Carruthers grabbed a hold of the dangling handcuffs, while Bumble lost his balance and toppled over. He scrambled frantically to try and grab the tie down ring but missed. Gravity did the rest.

Carruthers watched helplessly as Bumble tumbled towards the open door. He was going to fall out of the plane! Bumble's instincts took over. He reached out and grabbed hold of the canister, squeezed his eyes shut, and held on with all of his might as they both slid out of the plane.

16

Aftershocked

The next five seconds were the longest five seconds of Bumble's life. He clung to the top of the canister with white knuckles and held his breath. Then came the wonderful sound of his parachute opening, followed by the graceful upwards tug as it filled with air.

He sighed in relief and opened his eyes to see *Eightball Charlie* flying away, and looked down to see a large and flat rock formation coming up fast beneath him. The canister hit the rocks sharply with a loud CLANG and flopped over onto its side. Bumble went flying as the top of the canister popped off and was pulled away by the billowing parachute. The canister rolled to the water's edge but thankfully no further and stayed on the dry rock. Bumble came to rest on some kind of soft mossy growth, and finally feeling solid earth under him, let out a loud groan, and collapsed in relief.

As he lay there catching his breath, he could hear *Eightball Charlie* fly away into the distance, until before long, it was gone. Then there was only the peaceful sound of waves gently lapping against the rocks. Up in the sky, the rain clouds parted slightly and the sun appeared. It felt warm and comforting, like a blanket. Bumble took off his canteen helmet, closed his eyes and fell asleep almost immediately.

Meanwhile, back on *Eightball Charlie*, Carruthers closed the cargo hold door and made his way up into the cockpit as Crash turned the wheel towards home and revved the engines to full throttle. Carruthers dropped down into the Captain's chair and rubbed his sore wrist where the handcuffs had cut into his skin.

"How did we do?" asked Crash.

"Not great. The canister landed safely on one of the bigger rocks, so at least it's where it's supposed to be. That's the good part..."

"What, there's more?"

"Yes. Sorry, hate to tell you, but we lost our little friend out the door when we tipped. He's gone."

"What?!" Crash was shocked, then devastated. "Oh...Bumble..." was all he could say.

That little mouse had saved the mission, and probably their lives. Despite his fear, he was brave and courageous and did what he had to do when it counted most, and look where it got him. It was terrible. Crash shook his head and thought about what to do. He turned to Carruthers.

"Get on the radio. Tell them what's happened. 'Radio silence' my foot!" He thumped the glare panel with his fist in frustration. "This whole thing has been a disaster!" Carruthers got up, crossed over to the radio operator's station and turned it on. He flipped a few selector switches and turned the main dial – the lights on the control box lit up, but there was no sound. All he could hear was a faint and very distant hiss but no real signal.

"We've got another problem. The radio's out."

"Check the back of the box, make sure all the connectors are hooked up…"

Carruthers looked around the back of the radio, and saw the problem immediately. The circuit breaker had been removed from the back of the panel.

"The main copper connector is gone. Looks like someone pulled it out prior to the flight." He looked in the supply box. "No spares."

It was yet another crafty bit of sabotage, and although it was only a small connector, it presented a big problem. They needed a working radio, especially now after all that had happened. Crash tried to concentrate. How do you fix a radio with a missing copper connector with no replacement copper connectors on board? He felt the answer was right in front of him.

Out of the corner of his eye he glimpsed the empty canteen clipped to the Captain's chair and again thought of Bumble, and how he courageously used the cap as a helmet – wait – that was it! Bumble found his old lucky penny back at the base – and the lucky penny was solid copper! Crash reached into his pants pocket.

"Ha! That's right! Lucky Penny!" he yelled as he pulled it out of his pocket. "Here – use this!"

He flipped it in the air. Carruthers caught it and slid it into the connector plate. It fit like a glove. This time, as he turned the dial, he heard all the signals loud and clear. The radio was fixed. He gave Crash the thumbs up, turned the dial to Station 102, pushed the microphone switch and started talking.

The control tower at Station 102 was mobbed. News of the connector rings' discovery and of Davenport's role in the station's sabotage had spread around the base like wildfire. Everyone was crowded along the back wall, just outside the door, or up along the staircase, waiting to hear any reports of *Eightball Charlie*'s whereabouts and well-being.

Chief sat right behind Wisniewski, while Ed and Fred paced nervously along the windowsill. After a careful search of the entire base, they had not found their friend Bumble anywhere, and had concluded that he must have been aboard the flight. Then, the radio crackled to life.

"Station one-oh-two this is *Eightball Charlie*, come in, over. Station one-oh-two this is *Eightball Charlie*, come in, over."

As Carruthers' voice came in on the speaker, the room erupted into shouts of relief and excitement. Wisniewski waved his hand for everyone to quiet down and replied, "This is Station one-oh-two. We read you *Eightball Charlie*, what is your status?" The room got very quiet as everyone leaned in to hear more clearly.

"Station one-oh-two, mission failed.   Repeat, mission failed."

Everyone gasped. Wisniewski looked at Hammond and spoke again into the microphone.

"*Eightball Charlie*, please clarify."

"Station one-oh-two, secret cargo dropped over Jersey Island in error. Captain Davenport deserted aircraft, bailed out with main crate.   Smaller secondary canister successfully dropped over Minkies, along with a mouse. Heading back to base now."

Chief looked at Ed and Fred with wide eyes.   Poor Bumble! As the radio chatter continued, Chief pushed his way out of the room and the mice quickly followed.

Outside, they met Mortimer and filled him in on all of what they had just heard. They all felt sick to their stomachs.

"Well this is a very unsatisfactory turn of events..." said Mortimer when they were done.

"Bumble, lost..." said Ed.

"I just can't believe it." said Fred.

"Well *I* can." said Chief. "Bumble's my best buddy! And my Person…he's a two-faced snake. How could I have not seen it? How could I have been so blind? Oh I'd like to bite his leg!"

"Well actually, dogs admire their owners, without question. It's genetic. It's not you." said Ed.

"A very unsatisfactory state of affairs." Mortimer repeated.

"Yes Mortimer, we know that!" exclaimed Chief. "But what do we do?"

"Well obviously we need to launch a rescue expedition," said Fred.

"Ah, yes, a rescue! That would be glorious!" agreed Mortimer.

Chief was beside himself. "And just how do you all propose we do that? Bumble – *if* he's alive – is marooned on a rock somewhere out in the middle of the English Channel, all by himself."

Mortimer agreed. "You make a good point. We *are* somewhat landlocked here, but have no fear, we shall activate the network and put the word out. Don't worry old boy, we'll get him back." Mortimer patted his claw on Chief's paw sympathetically, and took off underground.

Chief gulped. He looked so sad.

"Don't you worry about Mister Bumble, he's very resourceful," said Ed.

"And clever," added Fred to Ed's irritation.

"That's what I said. Resourceful means clever."

"No, resourceful means talented and inventive. Clever means intelligent and skillful."

"He's all of the above. All of the above," sighed Chief. And that was simply all there was to say about that.

Meanwhile, in an open field somewhere on the island of Jersey, Davenport finished his fourth cigarette and checked his watch. A German cargo truck appeared over the crest of a nearby hill, stopped and turned on its lights. Davenport pulled a flashlight from his flight suit and flashed it twice quickly. The truck drove towards him in reply.

Davenport stood up and stretched. Sitting on the crate had made his rear end sore. He looked at the big box and smiled. His German handlers would be proud. With any luck, they will bring it – and him – all the way to Berlin to analyze it. Jersey was only a small island. Bigger things were happening elsewhere, and he was sure he would finally be a part of them.

The truck pulled up and two men jumped out and loaded the crate into the back. Davenport climbed into the front cabin, lit another cigarette and smiled. They drove off towards Island Headquarters. Mission accomplished.

Eightball Charlie meanwhile, flew safely north to the coast of England. It was a miracle that they hadn't been spotted by any enemy fighters. Carruthers sat up front in the pilot's chair and enjoyed the view. The familiar green countryside was a welcome sight for the exhausted Crash McCormick. He knew how lucky they were to have made it this far in one piece. Perhaps their previous string of bad luck was finished now that the mission was over. All that was left to do was to get *Eightball Charlie* down on the ground safely at Station 102.

But in the back of his mind, Crash couldn't shake what Bumble had said about the missing hydraulic connector ring. Bumble must have climbed up through the wheel wells and would have been in the perfect position to find anything suspicious. If *Eightball Charlie* had been leaking hydraulic fluid this whole time, several serious things could still go very wrong. As a precaution, Crash decided to lower the landing gear early, and when he pushed the "Gear Down" button, instead of hearing the comforting sound of the landing gear motors whirring into action, there was only silence. He looked at the landing gear pressure gauge, and there was no reading. The needle was stuck at zero. Then, right on cue, the red "Landing Gear Unsafe" light lit up. Bumble was right again. The gear wasn't down, nor was it going to drop on its own. He set the landing gear selector control to NEUTRAL.

"How's that wrist of yours?" Crash asked Carruthers.

"Fine, better, why?"

"Because it's about to get a workout. See that thingy down there?" Crash pointed to a handle on the floor at the bottom of the seat. "That's the emergency hand crank for the landing gear. Start cranking!"

"Blast!" Carruthers reached down, grabbed hold and started turning. This was the first time the emergency hand crank had ever been used on *Eightball Charlie*, so it was extremely stiff. Crash looked in the flight manual.

"According to this, it should take fifty turns to get one wheel down. One hundred for both, counter-clockwise."

"Great. Wonderful. Thank you."

Carruthers cranked the little wooden handle. After only about ten turns, he began to sweat from the effort, and his hand and wrist started to cramp.

"This is fun," he grunted. "At least I'll be able to make some kind of contribution to the mission. I've been about as useful as a wooden frying pan so far. Today has not exactly been my best performance."

"Mine neither. But you just got here. You have an excuse. Me? I knew the guy, or at least I thought I knew him, and he played me – played all of us – like a fiddle. Fake orders, fake map, fake friend. I don't know which makes me feel worse, the fact that he got away with the box, or that Bumble saved us only to get hurled out of the plane."

"Yes, I'm very sorry about that. Seemed like a nice little chap. That was my fault."

"It's not your fault, I tipped the plane too soon. If it's anybody's fault it's Davenport's. I just hope Bumble's alright."

"Me too."

As Carruthers turned the crank, ever so slightly on the underside of the plane, the landing gear started to move.

A short while later, *Eightball Charlie* finally got within sight of Station 102. Carruthers' hand and wrist ached from all the cranking, but the landing gear was finally down and locked, much to their relief. A few thousand feet out, Crash pushed forward on the control wheel to begin their descent and extended the landing flaps to slow their speed.

And unfortunately, the landing flaps didn't work either.

"Oh no!" gasped Crash.

"Now what?!" yelled Carruthers.

Crash frantically flipped pages in the flight manual and pointed to another emergency hand pump – this time, a big one on the side panel directly behind his copilot's chair.

"There's not enough hydraulic fluid left to operate the landing flaps. Grab that thing on the wall and start pumping! Fast!"

Carruthers jumped up, grabbed the pump with both hands and started pumping with all of his might. It was like rowing a boat with a spoon.

"I hate this plane!" he screamed.

"Oh I love her! I love her 'cause she's going to get us home in one piece! Aren't you sweetheart?!" Crash petted the glare panel gently.

Outside, under the wing, the flaps started to open and slowly drop down into place. The change in speed could be felt almost immediately, which was a good thing, because the runway was coming up fast.

"It's working!"

"Good! But I still hate it!"

Crash leveled the plane out and dropped the engine's speed. She drifted in, and after a few last frantic pumps from Carruthers, she touched down on Runway Two. To their great relief, the landing gear held.

But *Eightball Charlie* had one last surprise left.

When Crash applied the brakes, they didn't respond, as they too were powered by hydraulics. Crash groaned as he stomped on the brakes with both of his feet and all of his might. Carruthers jumped into the pilot's seat and did the same. Both men's faces grimaced with effort as *Eightball Charlie* raced down the runway.

They pushed and pushed, and every last drop of hydraulic fluid left in the plane finally made its way to the brakes. The plane slowed, the cockpit shook furiously, and Crash cut the engines, revved them in reverse and after a few hundred feet, *Eightball Charlie* eventually…finally…came to a complete stop.

Crash's hands shook as he let go of the wheel. Carruthers rubbed his wrists and wiped his brow. The propellers chugged to a stop. Both men breathed heavily as the engine noise whined down and the cockpit was once again silent and serene.

After a moment, Crash turned to Carruthers and repeated the catchphrase he had heard a thousand times before, but never really understood or appreciated until today.

"All's well that lands well."

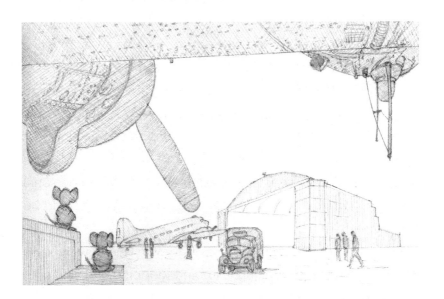

17

Marooned On The Minkies

After a nice long nap, Bumble yawned and had a big stretch. He breathed deeply and took in the sea air. The sun had come out and the sky was now a beautiful blue. And most of all, it was quiet. After everything that had happened on *Eightball Charlie*, Bumble appreciated the simple quiet. The propeller vibrations had been bone shaking, the howling wind of the open cargo door had felt like a hurricane and the spinning starboard wheel of doom was an experience sure to give him nightmares for years to come.

Bumble was very grateful to be in one piece, safe and dry on the Minkies. Or relatively dry anyway. While he was asleep the tide had come in, and water lapped against his feet and the end of his tail. He stood up and looked around. This particular rock was several yards square, and felt like a personal island. He wondered how long he would be here. It could be some time.

He stretched again. Muscles everywhere were sore from all of the frantic running, climbing, gripping and falling he had done this morning. If you had asked him when he woke up today if he ever imagined that he would wind up here, on this desolate rock, alone before lunch, he would have said no.

"Not in a million years!" he said to no one in particular.

Which brought up an important point. Lunch. Bumble was starving, and his stomach rumbled in agreement. By the looks of the sun's position and the rising waters of the tide, it was probably mid to late morning. He had been up since early daybreak and hadn't eaten a crumb all day. Bumble turned his attention to the open canister. There had to be *some* kind of food in there.

It was half under water, and most everything inside was wet – except for one very small package within easy reach at the top of the canister. By some miracle, it was still completely dry. Whatever it was, it was probably among the last items put in there before the canister was sealed. The package was very light and wrapped in wax paper. In another few minutes the rising tide would get to this too, so Bumble hefted it up onto his shoulders, carried it out and set it down on the rock. He unwrapped the package to find a small box of French stamps.

"Ah...postage stamps...perfect! Not much use out here, but a wet stamp is a ruined stamp. Maybe I'll keep one. Frame it and hang it on my living room wall. If I ever get *back* to my living room, that is." He pushed the box of stamps up to the highest point on the rock.

He went back into the canister and found several soggy sheets of writing paper, brought them out to dry and laid the box of stamps on top of them to keep them from blowing away. Next he found a wet box of waterproof matches. "Ah...now THESE I need! Excellent!"

After several trips, Bumble was able to collect a needle and thimble, a spool of thread, a few buttons, a package of chewing gum, a piece of chalk, a cigarette lighter and a small box of razor blades.

After all of the collecting, Bumble was even hungrier than before, and was very disappointed that he hadn't found any food in the canister. No crackers, no cheese, no nothing. It would be about 5 hours before the tide was low enough for him to get down to the bottom of the canister, and besides, whatever he found in there would have been soaked in salt water that whole time. If there *were* cans of food, his trusty shovel *might* be able to puncture the metal, so he had to just sit tight and wait for the tide to go back out. Well, he needed to lose weight anyway. Skipping a meal wouldn't kill him. He patted his tummy and stuck his thumbs in his belt, and realized with horror that his shovel wasn't there – it was gone – and he remembered that he left it stuck in the handcuffs locked on Corporal What's-His-Name's wrist. Now, even if he did find a can of food, he had no way to open it.

"Fibblejibbits!" he groaned out loud to no one in particular, and flopped down on his butt in disappointment.

Bumble got grumpy if he waited too long to eat. His mother used to say his father got "hangry" or "hungrumpy" if dinner wasn't ready when he got home. Now Bumble knew what she meant. His stomach again rumbled in agreement.

He sighed and looked over at the items spread out on the rock. Out in the sun, everything had begun to dry quickly, and then, very unexpectedly, something interesting happened. Bumble's nose picked up a scent. Believe it or not, something smelled like food. He sniffed the air again. Yes, something definitely smelled like food. What could it be? He smelled each item. When he got to the paper, his eyes widened.

"Rice!" he exclaimed.

It was rice paper. And rice paper, you could eat. Bumble was thrilled! He tore a corner off one of the sheets and touched his tongue to it. It tasted a little salty from the salt water, but not too salty. He took a small bite and chewed it. It was stiff and crunchy, like a cracker. He licked his lips and then dug in happily. He chomped and chomped, tore another piece off and chomped some more. Before long he had gobbled up about a third of the sheet and burped a loud and satisfied burp. But all that salty rice paper had made him thirsty. He looked around and saw a deep crack in the rock filled with water. Luckily it had rained earlier that morning, so there were puddles of fresh rainwater everywhere, filling all the nooks and crannies around the rock. He had read stories of men drinking seawater and dying, and was in no hurry to try it for himself.

He grabbed the thimble and walked over to the puddle, dipped it in and took a nice long drink of refreshing rain water.

"Ahhhhhh...that's lovely."

He looked down at the puddle, about to scoop up another thimbleful of water, when he noticed his reflection. He was still filthy from the soot in *Eightball Charlie*'s starboard engine. What a mess.

"Ooooooh…that's not so lovely."

He trotted over to the water's edge, and out of habit looked around to make sure that he was alone, then stripped out of his mechanic's jumpsuit. He whistled as he tiptoed into the ocean, and using the thimble as a bucket, began to wash. The water was cold and his big teeth chattered, but he was happy to be getting clean. A little minnow swam by and disappeared into some nearby seaweed.

In the far distance he could see the faint outline of warships. He wondered what type they were, and whether they were British or German. It was impossible to tell. They certainly couldn't see him.

He didn't know how long he would be stuck out here, and thought he should probably start to take steps towards being seen by the outside world in some way. Perhaps he should use those matches he found and burn something to create a smoke signal. The inside of canister smelled like wet wool, so there had to be clothing or a blanket or something in there that could be burned. But then again, he might need that cloth to make some sort of bed for tonight, and perhaps the night after, and the night after that. His mind wandered into the future, and he saw himself with a long beard, looking like a sun-crazed castaway, talking to himself and dancing on the rock. Best not to let that happen.

Finally clean, Bumble snapped his fingers as he remembered his dirty jumpsuit. He scrubbed it against the dimples on the outside of the thimble to get out the more stubborn splashes of oil, and laid it out in the sun to dry.

He again thought about rescue and looked at his collection. His eyes settled on the piece of chalk, and he smiled. He could write a message that could be seen from the air! Of course, it was so simple.

"Ha!" he said as he picked it up. But what to write? His rock wasn't that big, so a sentence was out. It had to be short and sweet, but big and readable at the same time. He was in international waters, so he needed to think of something that was common to every language. This was a challenge. As he sat down to give it more thought, he tapped the chalk on the rock. Tap tap tap. Tap tap tap. Without realizing it, he started tapping out the Morse code he had learned the night before in

Crash's room. Wait – that was it – Morse code! He remembered reading that the international signal for help was S.O.S. – why not simply write *that* on his rock! It was short, could be written large, and was internationally recognized.

"Splendid!" he exclaimed. He jumped up and started sketching.

After about an hour, the first "S" was finished. It probably measured a full yard from top to bottom. Not too bad.

But in that time, the sun had positioned itself directly overhead, and it had gotten very hot. Bumble would have to pace himself. Also, it had to be around lunchtime, so he set down the chalk and tore off another piece of rice paper for lunch. He sat inside the canister to enjoy some cool shade and started nibbling. In the distance, he watched a flock of seagulls swarm above a pack of fish flapping at the surface of the water. The tide must finally be going out. He took a big gulp of water from the thimble and got back to work.

Another long hour passed, and the "O" was done. Bumble hoped it was round enough, but it would have to do, whatever it looked like. The chalk was now worn down to just a small stump, and there wasn't enough to even begin the second "S", so Bumble decided to leave the signal alone. Now that it was low tide, it was time to explore the bottom of the canister. Suddenly his carefree day on the rock had become very busy, and time was flying by. Bumble had to make the most of it.

He put on his jumpsuit and walked into the canister. Immediately, he found what had caused the wet wool smell – a bunch of loose caps. *A lot of help these will be* he thought, but at least they were small, and he might be able to pull one out by spearing it with the needle and thread. He climbed further into the canister and towards the bottom discovered one box of bullets, several cans of precooked ready-to-eat meat, and a container labeled DETONATORS, which he decided not to touch. There were loose batteries scattered everywhere, a flashlight and a Swiss Army style pocketknife. He crouched behind one of the batteries – pushed – and rolled it like a barrel right out of the canister. After a few trips, he had managed to roll enough of them out to power up the flashlight. Then he turned his attention to the pocketknife. It was very heavy, and he wasn't even sure he could pull the blade open once he got it out of the canister.

The truth was, Bumble was exhausted, and the events of the day were finally catching up with him. He was overwhelmed and over-tired. He wasn't thinking clearly, and his emotions took over. All of a sudden, he was scared. He was scared that he would run out of paper to eat, or rainwater to drink, that he might be trapped on this rock forever, and that he might even die here, and never make it back home. He sat down and put his head in his hands.

About a quarter of a mile away to the east, a low-flying formation of dragonflies were searching for the *Eightball Charlie* cargo, and they were headed straight in Bumble's direction. Dragonflies have large eyes with thousands of lenses in them, and can see almost a full three hundred and sixty degrees, which makes them ideal for search and rescue missions. Their four wings allow them to fly forwards, sideways, backward or to hover in place, and they can fly at speeds of up to thirty miles per hour, among the fastest in the insect kingdom. Their only limitation is their short life spans, which make them want to complete their missions with all the more energy and enthusiasm.

This group was no exception. Squadron Leader Dudley Jones called out to the rest of the dragonfly team. "Look sharp!" he said. "Somewhere down there is the whatever-it-is we're looking for. We can't afford to miss it. So look sharp!"

Dragonfly Number 2 answered, "Yes, you told us that, didn'tcha?"

Truth be told, Dudley didn't have the best working relationship with his team. They thought he was dense and felt he repeated himself too often. As a result, they were annoyed with much of what he had to say. He wasn't dumb of course, he was just enthusiastic, and kept right on repeating himself to make sure the mission instructions were clear. After all, there was a war on, and they weren't there to make friends.

The formation raced ahead, with every member scanning every rock they passed over. There were only a few hours of daylight left and lots of ground left to cover. So far, they had seen nothing. Dudley explored a new train of thought with the others.

"Someone should come up with a numbering system for all these rocks out here. HQ could plug them into the grid, then check them off against what we've seen and calculate what still needs to be counted. How many rocks *are* there? How do we know? Someone should come up with a numbering system."

As expected, no one responded. Dudley continued.

"A numbering system would make our search less confusing, and shorten the number of hours we spend. We're in a time sensitive situation, and a numbering system would make our time out here more productive."

"So?" asked the youngest dragonfly of the group, Number 5.

Dudley was insulted. "So?? What do you mean 'So'? What I've said makes perfect sense! That's out of line Number Five!"

"That's not what I meant, Sir. Look – down there – written on the rock – the word 'So'."

Dudley looked and saw Bumble's incomplete S.O.S.

"Ah Ha! Brilliant Number Five! Brilliant! That's it – that's what we're looking for! Well done!"

The formation slowed and buzzed around Bumble's rock to get a closer look at the canister. Inside, Bumble was wiping away a tear when Dudley hovered down into view. Bumble's eyes went wide.

"Ha! I'm saved!!" Bumble shrieked, much to Dudley's surprise.

"Indeed you are!" Dudley answered. Bumble composed himself and walked out. The dragonflies all hovered at eye level and faced Bumble in formation.

"Squadron 655, The Black Dragons, at your service..."
Dudley said proudly, and saluted with his long spindly right
front leg.

"Bumble Humblestone, formerly of The Tire Tread Task
Force, at yours." Bumble replied, not knowing what else to say.
He returned the salute.

"Tire Tread Task Force? All the way out here? By the
looks of things, you must have had quite an adventure."
Dudley spun in place and faced the squadron. "Men, report
back to H.Q. Give them our position. Tell them we've found
the cargo and an agent. We will wait for here for pickup
tomorrow. And mention to them my idea of numbering these
islands for the next time..."

The squadron buzzed in reply, rose up in formation and
flew back in the direction from which they had come. As
Bumble watched them fly away, Dudley landed softly next to
him.

"Breaking in some new recruits. You know how it is.
They need to be told things over and over until it sinks in. Thick
skulls. So, my dear man, do you have anything to eat on this
island of yours?"

"Yes."

"Splendid. Any insects by chance?"

"Ah, no I'm afraid not."

"No? Oh dear. Are you sure there aren't any small
creepy-crawlies sharing this island with you? Believe me, I'm
not picky. I love mosquitoes, gnats, bees, flies, termites or ants
equally..."

"You are free to look, but I don't think so."

Dudley was disappointed. All that flying had made him
very hungry.

"I can offer you rice paper." Bumble said with a smile. "Or peppermint chewing gum."

Dudley considered his options. "No, that's alright. I'll eat when the fishing boat picks us up. Lots of flies on those boats! Mmmmmm."

"Fishing boat?"

"Yes. The Resistance often disguise themselves as fishermen to move out here on the water. Considering some of them actually were fisherman before the war broke out, it is a very easy part for them to play-act."

Bumble was impressed. He was also greatly relieved.

"Thank you for finding me," he said.

"Think nothing of it! There's a war on – we've all got to do our part. This container of yours must mean something to somebody to send us out here looking for it."

"Well, that is a bit of a story I am afraid. The actual something someone is looking for was stolen by someone else. *This* container was only a secondary supply drop, nothing more."

"And yet you have saved the many items that I see here. Give yourself some credit, Mr. Bumble Humblestone of the Tire Tread Task Force."

Dudley buzzed over, looked at the items and stopped at the chewing gum.

"On second thought, why don't I give one of these a chew? Can you help me with this, seeing that I don't have any thumbs?"

Bumble opened the packet of gum and laid out a stick for Dudley to sample, which he did happily.

"While we wait, tell me your story. Real stories are the most interesting ones, you know. I have a few of my own which may not completely bore you." Dudley blew a bubble with a loud POP.

And with that, Bumble sat down on the book of stamps and told Dudley everything that had happened up until this point. Dudley was fascinated, and the time passed quickly.

They talked all through the afternoon and well into the night. The last story Bumble remembered before falling asleep was one from Dudley, and had something to do with the development of a new flying machine that could hover in place, fly backwards and sideways, and go straight up and down, just like a dragonfly. Something called a "helicopter". Bumble wondered whether Dudley was making it up but was too tired to ask.

18

Voyage To *The Vigilant*

Early the next morning, Bumble woke to the chug-chug-chug of an approaching boat engine. He and Dudley had stayed up most of the night, and when it finally came time for some shut-eye, Bumble discovered that dragonflies buzzed in their sleep. Loudly.

"So much for that..." he said as he yawned and rubbed his eyes. He had a headache from lack of sleep. Dudley, still deep asleep, buzzed and twitched with a big grin on his face. Telling tales had done him some good. Who knew dragonflies led such spirited lives?

Bumble looked across the water to see a fishing boat. A man stood in the front jabbing a very long pole into the water, pushing the boat away from the shallow rocks. Bumble waved his hands excitedly.

"Ah-Ha!"

Dudley woke up at Bumble's yelling.

"What? What? Are we there yet?"

"Look Dudley – they've found us – just as you said they would!"

"Well of course they found us..." he said, yawning. "My squadron gave them our precise location! If only they would number these rocks though..."

The fisherman up front spotted the canister, turned to his partner up in the crow's nest on the top of the boat, whistled loudly and pointed at Bumble's rock. The other fisherman nodded and turned off the engine. The boat drifted in close, and the first man eased over the railing and jumped out to pick up the canister. As he stepped onto the rock, he could see the "S.O." chalk writing and neatly organized items, all of which he found very strange, until Bumble walked into view and started waving to him. The fisherman almost jumped out of his skin.

"Un petit souris!" he said ("a little mouse!"). The fisherman was quite amazed. But then he put it all together, and could see that this little mouse had gone through a great deal of effort to pull all of what he could from the flooded canister.

"Merci!" he said, tipping his cap.

Bumble smiled proudly.

"Bonjour! Comment allez-vous, Monsieur?"

Bumble didn't understand. He tilted his head.

"Parlez-vous français? Est-ce que tu me comprends?"

Bumble shrugged and shook his head "no". The fisherman scratched his chin and studied Bumble's jumpsuit and boots. A small flag on Bumble's shoulder gave it away.

"Hmmm. English?"

Bumble nodded "yes" and smiled again.

"Ah, bien sûr. I am Oliver. That is Sebastian." He pointed to the other fisherman. Sebastian did not seem very interested. Oliver turned his attention back to Bumble who extended his tiny hand for a shake. Oliver bent down and extended his pinkie finger. As they shook, Oliver looked around and was very impressed.

"This is quite extra-ordinary Monsieur Mouse. You are to be commended on your resourcefulness. I see many items here that you have saved from the salt water. Well done. Very well done indeed. Now, may I ask, inside this container, did you see detonators?"

146

Bumble nodded "yes".

"And ammunition?"

Another "yes" nod.

"And spare parts for a radio transmitter?"

Bumble shook his head "no".

"That's alright, not to worry. But now we must go. Back to dry land, yes?"

Bumble nodded "yes" excitedly.

Oliver turned to Sebastian, and yelled at him to come down and help, which he did, reluctantly. Bumble waved hello, but Sebastian hardly looked at him as he cut the parachute free and set the loose top back on top of the canister. Then together the men heaved it onto the back deck with a loud CLANG. *Maybe Sebastian didn't want to get wet...* Bumble thought.

They tipped the contents out onto the deck. Sebastian took the pocketknife, Oliver the flashlight. They tossed the wool caps into the cabin and split the cans of mystery meat between them for lunch. The detonators and the ammunition were gently placed into the bottom of a bucket. Sebastian then dumped a bunch of fish into the bucket to make sure they were hidden. They opened a secret panel in the floorboards and slipped the empty canister inside. Canisters like that came in handy for other dangerous uses, like loading them with TNT and turning them into makeshift bombs.

Oliver came back and collected Bumble's rescued items. He took the stamps, the lighter, the gum – everything – and placed them all in his shoulder bag. Bumble smiled.

"Ready to go?" Oliver asked. Bumble nodded excitedly.

Oliver put out his hand. "Okay Monsieur Mouse. Up you go." *Every time I hear that,* Bumble thought to himself, *look where it gets me.* He marveled at the irony. He climbed up into Oliver's hand and took one last look at his private island. As Oliver lifted him up, he saw the "S.O." and shook his head.

I wish I had had more chalk... he thought. Then he turned and looked at the boat. It was very crusty looking, covered in chipped paint and rust. What a perfect decoy. Bumble saw Dudley happily buzzing around a group of flies that were themselves buzzing around the bait station. Oliver let Bumble down on the deck, whistled loudly to Sebastian and yelled "Allons-y!" ("let's go!"). Sebastian nodded from up in the crow's nest and started the engine, while Oliver took his position in the front and used the pole to push the boat back and away from Bumble's rock. The engine chugged as they slowly reversed out of the clog of rocks.

Bumble meanwhile had made his way over to the bait station. It was a horrid and messy place covered in fish guts and scales, and it turned Bumble's stomach to even get near it. Dudley however was very happy, as he had already caught enough flies to satisfy him for the full day. Bumble held his nose.

"So Dudley, are you coming with us to the mainland?" he asked, sounding very nasally.

"No, I'm afraid not, my friend. Have to meet up with the squadron. The next adventure awaits. For you too, I'm sure. There's a war on you know, we've all got to do our part. Every day counts."

"Yes, I suppose so," Bumble answered. He was disappointed his new friend wouldn't be coming along, and the thought that he may never see Dudley again weighed heavily on him. Dragonflies had such terribly short life spans. It was cruel to make such a nice friend only to lose him. With a lump in his throat Bumble said, "Thank you again for finding me Dudley Jones of Squadron 655, The Black Dragons – I owe you a lot. More than you know."

"Think nothing of it. Line of duty and all that sort of thing." He could see Bumble was sad to see him go. "Chin up, little mouse. Remember our stories, they are the sum of our lives. I will tell yours. Don't forget mine. We are but vapor and dust... Farewell Bumble Humblestone of The Tire Tread Task Force!" And with that, Dudley hovered up into the air, gave Bumble a short salute, turned and flew off.

Bumble watched him fly away and disappear. "Goodbye..." he said, but he knew Dudley couldn't hear him. He wiped his eyes and collected himself. Time to move on to the next adventure, indeed. Free of the rocks, the boat turned east out into the open waters of the English Channel and headed towards German-occupied mainland France.

Meanwhile, at German HQ on Jersey Island, Davenport entered the office of Commandant Von Strum, the man in charge of the island. Behind him, two soldiers brought in the Top-Secret Resistance Communications Device and set it on the Commandant's desk. Now out of its crate, the impressive machine seemed like something from the future – a gleaming black metal spider. No one in the room had ever seen anything like it before. The Commandant smiled like a boy on Christmas morning.

"You have brought me the most extraordinary gift, Captain. You are to be commended. Actions such as yours do not go unrewarded by The Reich."

"Thank you," Davenport smiled.

"Shall we turn it on? See how it works?"

"By all means."

They both leaned in and looked around the machine for an "ON" switch, but didn't see one. Von Strum looked at Davenport, expecting he should know what to do. Davenport shrugged.

"I didn't build the thing. I just delivered it."

Von Strum grunted and walked around the back of the machine. He noticed the hand crank on the left side.

"It seems to be self-powered. Here, turn this crank." He pointed.

"Who, me?"

"Yes of course you! I'm the Commandant, I don't touch machinery of any kind!"

Davenport reached out and started turning the crank. The machine came to life. Lights started blinking. The radio started humming. Von Strum's eyes grew wide in excitement and ambition.

"Is it the new M-209 I wonder? We've heard the Americans were working on something...perhaps we can turn this into a *wunderwaffen* ("a wonder weapon").

"Like I said pal, I just delivered it."

"Hmmm. It looks even more complicated and sophisticated than our Enigma Machine. How wonderful to have one to ourselves. Again, you have done very well Herr Davenport."

"Thank you, Herr Commandant." Davenport smiled again. He reached over and turned the radio dial, extended the antennas and pushed a few of the buttons on the keyboard. The machine beeped and buzzed. It *was* doing *something*...but they had no idea what.

Ahead was the French coast. During the boat ride, Bumble had gotten to know Oliver a little bit, and Sebastian not so much. They were indeed members of The French Resistance, and were headed to their secret headquarters. They were part of a group called The Marquis – a very organized underground force that carried out all kinds of dangerous operations against the Germans.

The French Resistance was made up of regular people from all walks of life, and the actual resistance that occurred came in many forms. Farmers gave shelter and transport to downed British pilots, and helped smuggle them back to Britain. Factory workers made minor intentional mistakes in the manufacture of tools and equipment. Their flawed products resulted in long shortages and delays of needed supplies for the German army. With their local deliveries, shop owners carried forged documents, coded messages and identity papers. Postal workers sidetracked German mail and sent it to the British. Local churches handed out the underground press; printed reports of what was *really* going on under German occupation. Everyone worked together against the Germans.

And then there were The Marquis. They carried out only the most dangerous acts of sabotage. Sabotage that required dynamite. They blew up train tracks and electrical transformers. They chopped down telephone poles and cut the wires to interrupt German calls. They blocked roads to stop German troop movement. They were an army of freedom-fighters. Organized, patriotic and very effective. And it was this group that they were on their way to meet.

The fishing boat arrived at the beautiful coastal town of Barneville-Carteret. It looked now much like it did before the war, with the exception of German soldiers on the streets and swastika flags on the flagpoles. Sebastian muttered under his breath as they pulled into the harbor past a German Schnellboot – a motor torpedo boat the size of a large yacht. Bumble was starting to understand Sebastian's silence. He was one of those angry silent types, who stayed quiet until one day…they blew. Best not to be around him when he did.

Sebastian eased the boat up to the dock, and Oliver tied her down. A few German soldiers stood nearby, and Bumble couldn't help but stare at them. He had never seen German soldiers in person before. Living as sheltered and protected a life as he did at Station 102, he had spent his days focused on his job and on the goings-on at the base, but not so much on the outside world. Well here he was, out in the real world, and it was a very different and dangerous place.

Sebastian cut the engine and they prepared to leave the fishing boat. Oliver offered his hand to Bumble, lifted him up and dropped him in his front jacket pocket.

"Wait until you see where I am taking you, Monsieur Mouse. Somewhere *top secret*, as they say."

Oliver grabbed the shoulder bag with Bumble's items, while Sebastian grabbed the bucket of fish with the hidden detonators. They climbed out onto the dock and were immediately stopped by one of the German soldiers. Oliver tipped his hat, while Sebastian put on a big show, offering the soldier a fish from the bucket, telling him how fresh it is and how he should pick whichever one he liked. Of course, the soldier was revolted and sent them on their way, which was exactly what Sebastian thought he would do. The Germans were very predictable that way.

Once the soldier was gone, Bumble poked his head out from Oliver's pocket. He watched as they walked through the harbor entrance and up into the streets that ran along the water. Water taxis puttered along the canal, while people walked and bicyclists rode this way and that. The buildings were old and very pretty. Oliver and Sebastian turned onto a side street.

Up ahead was an ordinary-looking canal boat, a long narrow barge common to cities on the water, like London, Paris and Venice. On the stern was painted the name *Vigilant*. Sebastian quickly dumped the fish and delicately placed the detonators and ammunition into Oliver's open shoulder bag. The empty bucket got hooked onto a nearby pier post.

"Here we are, Monsieur Mouse," said Oliver, whispering. "*The Vigilant* – our secret base of operations, our moveable headquarters, able to take us wherever we are needed. Invisible, yet always on the move, right under their very noses. Spectacular, yes?"

Bumble nodded an impressed "yes".

On the outside it looked like any other canal boat, barely 7 feet wide and about 50 feet long, with windows along the main compartment every 10 feet or so. Once painted a beautiful midnight blue, years of exposure to the elements had now darkened it to an almost black. Oliver nodded to the lookout stationed at the bow, who waved back and rapped on the roof of the captain's compartment three times. The engine immediately fired up, and as the men stepped aboard, the boat pulled away from the dock and eased out into the canal. Sebastian opened the door to the cabin.

The interior of *The Vigilant* was indeed a floating headquarters. Bumble was amazed. The cabin was broken down into five sections, each of which had a man assigned to a different task. 'Maps and Cameras' was first. Here, photographs taken in secret by various Resistance operatives from all around France were blown up and analyzed, pinpointed on maps and given grid reference numbers. German buildings of every sort were cataloged and assigned different levels of importance. The plan was to blow them all up, eventually. Louis was in charge of maps and cameras. He wore thick glasses and was hunched over a particularly interesting photograph. He held it up to Oliver.

"Look there in the shaded area. Does that look like a tank to you? I think it's a tank..." Not waiting for an answer, he grabbed the picture back and put it under his magnifying glass before Oliver had a chance to really look at it.

Next came 'Forgery'. Here, identity papers and documents of every kind were copied with the greatest attention to every detail imaginable. Identification cards and fake passports were all hand-crafted to look as real as possible to the lazy or preoccupied German soldier's eye. There was a problem however, with these forgeries: identity numbers. The Resistance could only guess as to what numbers to use, and if the Germans ever checked up on a fake number and found it didn't exist, it led to a bad finish: interrogation, most likely followed by a firing squad. But don't tell that to Luc. Forgery was his station. Luc felt, not incorrectly, that his forgeries bordered on the quality of art. It wasn't his fault if the people using his handiwork couldn't talk their way past getting checked.

After 'Forgery' came 'Radio'. Here, a radio operator would listen for coded messages being broadcast on the radio during the French news. Seemingly innocent well wishes from someone's aunt or uncle were often mission instructions or valuable secret information. Once decoded, the operator was in charge of sharing this information with other groups across

France, usually through Morse code. There was a tapping key armature on the table next to the radio. Bumble perked up when he saw this, and he pointed excitedly.

"Yes...Morse code..." Oliver answered as they continued down the length of the boat. Sebastian sat down and put on the radio headset. This was his station. Now that they were back, he had a lot of work to catch up on.

Next, after 'Radio' came 'Props'. Here were found the brilliant disguises the Resistance used to stay one step ahead the Germans. Moustaches, bushy eyebrows, fake teeth, hats and makeup sat on a shelf. Pinned on the wall were color illustrations of all the different uniform rank insignia the Germans used. Different colors meant different ranks, while their Army, Air Force and Special Guard all used different symbols. It was all very complicated, and very different from how the Americans and British wore their ranks. On the desk Bumble saw several concealment devices, among them, a long skeleton key with a hollow shaft for messages, a lady's shoe with a secret heel compartment, and a jacket button that hid a miniature compass.

I could have used that button yesterday... Bumble thought.

'Props' was Oliver's section, which made sense, given his outgoing personality. They were almost at the front of the boat now. One section to go, and it was the most dangerous one.

Last, but certainly not least, after 'Props' came 'Explosives'. Oliver proudly handed the detonators to the man sitting there, named Michel, who seemed less than thrilled.

"Just once, I wish you would bring me parts that didn't smell like fish!" Michel said.

"Bah! What does it matter so long as they work?" was Oliver's reply. At Michel's station, Bumble could see detonators, charges and timers all in various states of readiness, and off to the corner of the desk, in small sausage-shaped parcels, were several rolls of plastic explosive. They looked harmless enough, like green putty wrapped in wax paper, but Bumble knew to keep his distance. It was very dangerous material. Bumble sniffed the air – the plastic explosive smelled just like almonds! His stomach rumbled loudly.

"Nobel's Explosive 808. The British drop it for us all the time. It's good stuff," Oliver said with a grin. Bumble couldn't get over how it smelled like almonds. That was the strangest thing to him. Michel got back to work, and Oliver opened the door to the forward compartment.

Inside was Antoine, who drove the boat. He was the best canal boat driver in the Resistance, but like the rest of the team, he was also a pretty prickly pear. He didn't even turn around as Oliver came in. He just puffed on his pipe.

"Finally back from Les Minquiers, eh Ollie? Did you find our precious cargo?"

"Yes and no. Mostly no. The big one got away. But my friend here managed to rescue these." Oliver reached into his shoulder bag and pulled out the book of stamps.

"Friend? What friend?"

Bumble popped up from Oliver's pocket and waved "hello".

Antoine chuckled to himself. "Ha! An English mouse! That's very good Ollie. A great deal of help I'm sure he'll be. All of our problems are solved. Thank you," he said sarcastically as he turned the wheel and puffed out a big cloud

157

of smoke from his pipe. Oliver handed the stamps to Bumble and set him down on the floorboards away from the captain's feet. Good thing he did, as just then the captain cleaned his pipe and knocked a big clump of smoky hot ash to the floor. Was he aiming for Bumble? Oliver shrugged and went back to his workstation.

Bumble coughed and sneezed, and then, from out of the smoke stepped the most beautiful white mouse he had ever seen. She looked closely at the stamps.

"I presume we have you to thank for these?" she said, and locked eyes with him.

Bumble was momentarily speechless. Dumbstruck. His mouth just dropped open, and only about half a squeak came out. He blinked and gulped and tried to gather himself. The pretty white mouse was enjoying his sudden bashfulness.

"My name is Marguerite. Marguerite La Fleur. And you are?" she extended her hand for a shake. He took her hand delicately.

"Bum…um…Bumble…Humble…um…" Bumble barely whispered.

"What's the matter? Cat got your tongue?" she said, and didn't immediately let go.

19

The Rodents Of Rouen
Have A Plan

When it came to female mice (especially the pretty ones), Bumble was your classic garden-variety mouse: shy, intimidated and hopelessly out of his league. Poor Bumble, he was so unprepared for the likes of Marguerite La Fleur. Lightning in a bottle, that's what she was.

He did have one thing going for him though, a tiny spark of oversized courage buried deep in his heart, and its still small voice that inspired him to inspect the flight map in Davenport's quarters, climb aboard *Eightball Charlie* at the very last second, and fix her starboard engine when they were sure to crash. And that still small voice wasn't just whispering, it was yelling at him, ordering him to "PAY ATTENTION!"

Pay attention indeed. How could he not? In her bright and shining eyes he saw fearless strength, courage and compassion. They were eyes he somehow immediately understood and trusted. This beautiful mouse had his full attention.

"So, we have you to thank for these?" Marguerite repeated, pointing to the stamps.

"Yes, they fell out of the airplane along with a bunch of other stuff. Including me. Ha ha. I kept them dry so they wouldn't stick together."

"Fantastique! Well I am very glad you did. They will be extremely useful. And so will you. I think it's time we leave these men to their work and go below deck. They've got a lot to do to prepare for tonight's mission, and we shouldn't get in their way."

"Mission? Tonight?" Bumble asked.

"Oh yes. Very exciting, you'll see. Do you like trains?"

"Trains? I love trains!"

"Good. Time to meet the rest of the team then."

"There's more?"

"Mmm-hmm. The Rodents of Rouen – the rats on the boat."

"Rats?" Bumble gulped.

"Oh yes. Better let them do the talking though. They may be a top sabotage squad, but they're a bit…guarded when meeting someone new."

"Understood. After you."

Bumble and Marguerite climbed down a hole in the floorboards to the narrow storage deck below. It was dank and dark, and at first it smelled like seaweed. But then the smell changed to something much better. In the middle of the storage compartment, Bumble saw a small wood-burning stove, like something from a little girl's dollhouse, and on that stove was a simmering pot of pot-au-feu, a classic French beef and vegetable stew. At a small table sat The Rodents of Rouen, the very same group of rats who were at The Red Lion Tavern back on Jersey Island. But instead of four, there were now only three of them. They were huddled together closely, spoke in hushed tones and looked at Bumble with suspicion. Marguerite meanwhile ran to the stove to check on her pot-au-feu.

"Not one of you could have stirred this while I was upstairs? Look, it almost burned! Thanks very much – for nothing – as usual!" She stirred the stew around and added a

161

little water to help loosen up the bits stuck to the bottom of the pan. She then dropped the book of stamps onto the table.

"He brings us these and you repay him by almost ruining his meal! Typical self-absorbed rats!"

"Rodents..." they mumbled.

"RATS!" she answered.

Bumble meanwhile cleared this throat and did his best to look tough, but he just came across as looking tired, which, truth be told, he was. The smell of Marguerite's pot-au-feu made him swoon.

"Give him a seat before he falls on his fanny!" said Number One. Number Two offered a chair. "For the seat of your pants, Monsieur."

"Many thanks." Bumble plopped down happily at the table and met their stares. They all studied each other saying nothing. Bumble swallowed hard and tried not to look at their scratches and scars. They were a tough bunch. Marguerite looked over her shoulder at the rats, rolled her eyes, sighed loudly and stirred the stew.

"Introduce yourselves! Must I do everything? Are you children?!"

The rats shook their heads at her constant nagging.

"I am Number One..." said Number One reluctantly.

"Two..." continued Number Two, while Number Three only held up three fingers and said nothing.

"No names. We use numbers instead. In case we are captured, tortured and forced to talk," Number One said soberly.

"We can't rat each other out if we don't know each other's real names," added Number Two. Number One shot him an angry look.

"Why must you say that? You know how that upsets me! 'Rat each other out...' Such a thoughtless thing to say."

"It's just a figure of speech," said Number Two, desperately.

"It's an insult!"

Number Three stared at Bumble and drew his index finger across his throat, made a sickening noise and stuck out his tongue, pretending to be dead.

Bumble was startled. At Station 102, the thought of capture and torture never even crossed his mind. It was a harsh reminder that he was indeed in the real world now. A heavy silence fell back over the table. Marguerite continued stirring the stew while everyone just stared at each other, sizing each other up, as if they were playing some kind of high-stakes card game.

Number One broke the silence.

"What do you know about locomotives?" he asked Bumble.

"Well, they get you from here to there I suppose, don't they?" Bumble answered cheerfully. Number Three grunted in disapproval. The icy stares continued, so Bumble decided to change his answer to something a bit more serious. "*Loco*, Latin for 'from a place' and *Motivus* for 'causing motion' – together make loco-motivus, or locomotion. Burning wood or coal in a steel boiler combustion chamber heats water and creates pressurized steam that then moves the train. Locomotives can haul anything anywhere at great speed, are incredibly strong, very dependable and monstrously huge." This answer seemed to be much more satisfactory.

"Monstrous indeed. Especially when they move soldiers and weapons, yes?" said Number One. Marguerite brought the pot-au-feu to the table. It was like something out of a dream.

"And that is why we must make sure they never leave the station…" she said as she grabbed several small plates, and started serving.

"How?" Bumble asked, genuinely intrigued.

"Why Dear, we're going to blow them up!" she said with a smile. "Now eat something."

She offered a plate to Bumble who was so surprised by what she said, how matter-of-fact she was about it, as if this was somehow all in a day's work, that for a moment he just stared at her. The rats served themselves and dug in hungrily, with lots of slobbering, slurping and gulping. Bumble however waited for Marguerite to sit down and serve herself. He ate one bite at a time, and wiped his mouth with a napkin, not his sleeve like the others. She gave them a dirty look.

"It's nice to have a *gentleman* around here – for a change!" she said. The rats ignored her and continued eating.

The pot-au-feu was the best meal Bumble could remember having in a very long time, since his mother had cooked for him actually. Looking across the table at this beautiful mouse, eating this delicious meal, Bumble came to realize something remarkable. He realized he was home. Ready or not, life was happening, right in front of him. It was time to pay attention, pay close attention to his heart, which, he quickly understood, meant following her. It was very clear. Just like that. This mouse's goose was cooked, so to speak. Bumble chuckled happily to himself.

"How do you like that!?" he said to no one in particular.

"Like what?" Marguerite asked.

"Oh. I'll tell you later..." Bumble said softly.

The rats had finished gobbling up their food and were now ready to get down to business. It was time for the plan. Number One got up from the table, put the pot back on the stove and crossed over to a shelf where he picked up several props and brought them to the table. He passed them out to Numbers Two and Three, and together they all assembled a scale model of a railroad station. They placed peanut shells on top of strands of dry spaghetti to represent locomotives waiting on their tracks. A saltshaker stood in for the switch tower, while brightly colored yarn tied around several pushpins represented the station's outer fence. Bumble was impressed. Marguerite folded her napkin and stood up as the rats sat down. She cleared her throat.

"Thank you, gentlemen. For the benefit of Monsieur Bumble, I am going to cover some of what you already know."

Bumble blinked twice. Marguerite was giving the briefing! She was the Team Leader! What an amazing mouse.

"Our objective is Le Gare De Port Bail – the train station in the town of Port Bail, a few miles to the south. Locomotives, as you have concluded Monsieur Bumble, are very valuable targets for us. We've recently learned that there will be several of them waiting at Port Bail for one night only – tonight – three troop transports and one ammunition train. They are supposed to leave first thing tomorrow morning." She pointed to the peanut shells.

"DEEESTROOY!" Number Three exclaimed as he thumped the table loudly. It was the first word Number Three had spoken since Bumble had arrived.

"Yes, thank you Number Three..." Marguerite said calmly. "If they get out of the station, over a thousand soldiers and untold numbers of weapons will be released into the world. If we can strike the locomotives *before* they leave the station, we can stop this from happening, or at least delay it for a good while. Locomotives are not easily repaired if sabotaged correctly. It takes months to fix them. Also, we're not in favor of directly killing anyone if we can avoid it. We're not murderers like them. Blowing up empty trains is morally acceptable, if there is such a thing in war."

She opened her jacket to reveal the Cross of Lorraine, the symbol of the French Resistance. It was a Latin cross with two horizontal beams instead of just one. The rats all nodded

and turned their collars up to reveal the same, and confirm their membership in this sacred brotherhood.

"Veritum Dies Aperit!" they all said in unison. Bumble translated the Latin in his head.

"Time Discovers The Truth..." he said. Marguerite nodded. Her tone was very serious.

"Yes. It always does. And time will reveal the truth of what the Nazis are really doing." They all sat in heavy silence for a moment before she continued.

"And now, how to blow them up. Oliver will impersonate an official train Inspector to get us inside the yard and close to the trains. He is upstairs sewing his uniform and practicing his German as we speak. There is a Superintendent in the yard who is a friend of the Resistance, and he will give Oliver a train-by-train tour. A small explosive charge placed deep inside the engine cylinders will cause the greatest damage. There is an access door along the main shaft of the locomotive, towards the front. The Superintendent will open each one and Oliver will place a magnetic plate bomb inside each as he "inspects" the inner workings. The magnet will stick securely to the inner wall. But, we have found out the hard way that the impact of setting the magnet in place is strong enough to set the bomb off if it's armed. That is why we are now 4 instead of 5."

She pointed to an empty chair at the other end of the table. The rats looked at it sadly. Bumble began to see the seriousness of their undertaking. Marguerite continued.

"Therefore, the magnetic plate bombs must be armed *after* they have been placed inside the locomotives. That's where we come in, one of us per train. Each explosive has a timer which will need to be set, giving us all enough time to make sure we get far away from the trains and out of the yard safely. Once the timer is activated, arm the bomb and get out of the locomotive. As we're operating at night, we'll have guards and searchlights to contend with, but not so many soldiers. Hopefully. Any questions?"

The rats shook their heads no, but Bumble raised his hand.

"What can I do to help? I'm very handy. I'm a mechanic you know. I could be useful, and by the looks of it you are one man short."

"What do you think? Should we let him come along?" she asked. They all murmured and shrugged. But Marguerite could see how genuine Bumble was in his offer to help, and she couldn't say no to this kind-hearted gentlemanly mouse who knew his Latin, had wonderful table manners and treated her like a lady.

"Well, you can be our lookout, how about that? Keep an eye out for any stray guards or anything suspicious. Can you whistle?"

Bumble stuck his fingers in his mouth and let out a loud screeching whistle. The rats covered their ears and winced. Marguerite was impressed.

"That will certainly work, Monsieur Bumble, thank you. That's our official 'we're in trouble' whistle. If you hear that, drop what you're doing…and *run*."

The rats all mumbled in agreement. Marguerite was ready to finish the meeting when Bumble raised his hand again.

"One more question."

"Yes?"

"Is there any more stew?" Bumble held up his empty plate. Marguerite smiled. The other rats grumbled, left the table, and headed back above deck.

"Here you are…" she said as she brought the pot back to the table and spooned out another plate for Bumble. He closed his eyes, took a big sniff and then dug in happily. Marguerite grabbed a crust of bread, pulled up a chair next to him and dunked her bread into his stew. Since she had done all the cooking she wasn't that hungry, but she enjoyed watching Bumble eat. They sat together quietly for a few more plates, until all of the stew was gone. Although she wouldn't admit it, Marguerite was beginning to feel quite at home with Bumble as well. This was shaping up to be quite a memorable day for both of them, but the day was far from over.

20

In Search Of Bumble

As *The Vigilant* made its way upriver towards the train station, Robin Winchester flew over the Minkies in search of Bumble. According to his original coordinates and the information from Chief and Mortimer, she was right where she needed to be, but the rocks all looked the same and they went on for miles in every direction. Little Bumble could be anywhere. A needle in a haystack or a mouse on a rock, take your pick, this was a big challenge. She found herself worried about poor Bumble too.

"Well, I'm sure the little guy's alright. He's just got to be! All alone out here by himself. It's simply awful. I hope I'm not too late..." she said to no one in particular.

Robin swooped high to low, left to right and right to left. Wispy eelgrass, a few broken shells here and there, some barnacles and seaweed were all that she could see on the rocks. Where was he? Where could he be?

Lucky for her it was mid-afternoon and the lowest point of low tide. After one dive that brought her down close over a bunch of very stinky mud, she swooped back up, shook her head to get rid of the disgusting smell and out of the corner of her eye, she glimpsed something white.

"Ah-HA!"

It was the submerged parachute from Bumble's canister. As she swooped over to get a closer look, she saw Bumble's incomplete S.O.S. signal and smiled.

"That's my mouse!"

She fluttered gently down and landed on Bumble's rock.

"Hello, Mister Bumble..."

She looked for him all around the rock, but it was deserted. Aside from a folded up chewing gum wrapper, a few shreds of what looked like paper, and a canteen top without a canteen, there was no sign of him. She was too late. Perhaps he drowned, or was eaten by a big fish or a passing seagull. How horrible. If only she had gotten there sooner. She scratched the rock with her talon sadly, and looked at the empty message tube on her leg and thought of Bumble's ink splattered coordinates. He was so brave. What could have become of him? She sighed heavily and prepared to take off when she heard a faint buzzing sound behind her. She turned to see a squadron of dragonflies flying low along the horizon, heading right towards her. As they grew closer, she heard the voice of the leader:

"...one hundred twenty-seven east, one hundred twenty-eight west...now make sure you mark these down...anyway, as I was saying, it was just up ahead that I found him. Most courageous little mouse I ever met. Remarkable story, actually. He had found some urgent information for the Resistance, and was able to pass it along with the help of his friends. A dog, a mole and –" he slowed when he saw Robin "– a beautiful white homing pigeon." The squadron came to a stop over Bumble's rock. Dudley Jones couldn't believe his eyes.

"This is extraordinary, utterly unbelievable! You are Robin Winchester, are you not? Carrier pigeon and associate of Bumble Humblestone the mouse?" Robin hopped up and down in excitement.

"Ha! You bet I am! How wonderful!"

"I must say you are even prettier in person than he described, Miss Winchester."

"Oh, I'm not. Well, maybe I am..." she batted her eyelids at the bugs. They all hovered in stunned silence. After an awkward moment, one of the team members cleared his throat. Dudley moved forward and tried to sound commanding.

"Ah, yes. Squadron 655, The Black Dragons, at your service Miss Winchester..." he said.

"Call me Robin."

"Yes. Miss Robin. Well, what brings you all the way out here? To 'Bumble's Rock', number one hundred and twenty-nine north." He motioned to the squadron behind him. "Write that down." He turned back to Robin. "Hard to believe it was

172

only yesterday that he and I were marooned here, desperate castaways in need of rescue. Well, he was, not so much me. But I felt it only right to keep him company, being a brother in arms and such. And so, I did. Until the rescue."

"Oh, thank Goodness! He's safe! Where is he?"

"Due east – in mainland France by now I should think. A Resistance fishing boat picked us up, and headed straight for the coast, for a meeting with *The Vigilant*, the Floating Fortress of Sabotage. Wish I could have been with him, but these rocks needed numbering you know…"

"Yes, so I see. Due east then?" Robin got ready to take off.

"Due east. *The Vigilant* is one of those long canal boats. Painted black for night missions. Almost invisible. Just follow the explosions, it won't be far away…" Dudley winked. Robin winked back.

"Thank you, Gentlemen, I am very grateful. Carry on. Until the next time…"

And with that, she bolted off into the sky in a hurry. Dudley and the boys watched her go, and when she disappeared into the distance, they resumed their rock counting.

"One hundred and thirty, west…one hundred and thirty-one south. Is someone writing these down?"

21

The Last Locomotive

The sun had set by the time *The Vigilant* drifted to a stop. They were about a mile from the train yard and the sabotage team would travel the rest of the way in a captured German Kubelwagon ("bucketcar"), which would arrive soon. *The Vigilant* had to keep moving, or it would be discovered. Once the group left the boat, they were on their own. *The Vigilant* would then blend in with the other water traffic and disappear.

Inside, final preparations were being made. Oliver buttoned up his German Officer's uniform and glued on a set of fake eyebrows. They helped get him into character to play the part of the Inspector, and he felt they made him look more commanding.

Sebastian tried to fit into his uniform but couldn't close the buttons. He muttered under his breath. He had put on weight, but it was too late to make any changes, so he would just have to suck in his gut and think thin.

Michel gave the explosive charges a final look, making sure they were firmly attached to their magnetic plates. They were. Under a magnifying glass he double-checked the wiring from the timers to the charges. Everything looked good. He – very carefully – placed them into Oliver's briefcase, one at a time, and delicately closed the latch.

Luc blew eraser shavings off of the just-finished fake identification papers and gently touched Oliver's photo to make sure the glue had dried. It had. The ID looked real – as long as you didn't look too closely. The ink signatures were dry, and he double-checked that it was today's date on the inspection papers. Everything looked good, and he handed them to Oliver with a nervous smile.

Marguerite, The Rodents and Bumble made their way up from below deck. They were dressed in black from head to toe. Bumble felt like a new mouse in this dangerous looking uniform. No grungy mechanic's jumpsuit for him anymore. He was now a select member of the team, on a top-secret mission of sabotage. And, more importantly, Marguerite thought he looked very handsome, which made his heart swell. This was quite a change, and he liked it.

Bumble kept his smile to himself however, as he could see the seriousness of the moment. This was the last time this particular team would be together. After the big mission, they would break up, go their separate ways and never see each other again. It helped cover their tracks. Other missions would bring new partners to carry on the fight. They couldn't afford to get too close to each other in case they got captured or interrogated. If someone honestly didn't know where any of their teammates were, that was good. If they didn't have any emotional ties to them, that was even better. Oliver stood at the back of the boat and spoke to the men.

"My friends, the time has come for us to strike a blow for freedom. Thank you for your courage. Thank you for your belief in a better day to come. Tonight, with any luck, these troops and their weapons will be stopped in their tracks, as we blast their locomotives to kingdom come!" The men clapped and nodded in agreement.

At the front of the boat, Marguerite addressed Bumble and the Rodents.

"As we go our separate ways tonight, please be as careful as you can. Be brave, but be smart. Be careful of who you trust. And each of you, take a few of these, and use them when you can. You know what addresses are safe, and you know the codes." She handed out all of Bumble's stamps – first to the Rodents, then the men. Bumble was surprised and happy to see them being given out, but saddened at the thought that these brave people should have had something so much better to work with. They deserved the Top-Secret Communications Device from London, but would have to settle for, and make do with, simple stamps. To make matters worse, the Germans had probably figured out how to use the Communications Device by now, and must be plotting against the Resistance in some way. Bumble shook his head in bitter disappointment.

"Fibblejibbits..." he murmured under his breath.

Outside, they heard the sound of a car horn. The Kubelwagon had arrived, right on time. The group took one last look at each other and everyone smiled bravely. They all saluted and said in unison, "Vive La France!" And with that, Oliver, Sebastian, the Rodents and the mice climbed out of the boat. In front of them, the car was running. The driver quickly lifted a bicycle out of the back seat and pedaled away. Sebastian climbed into the driver's seat while Oliver and company climbed into the back, where officers were supposed to sit. Sebastian turned on the lights, put the car into gear and they sped off down the road into the darkness. *The Vigilant* turned and motored away, its black hull invisible against the murky water. Within moments, both were gone. The operation was underway.

In the open back seat, Bumble breathed in the night air and looked at the stars. Marguerite nudged him and passed him a small piece of coal. She had used it to darken her face for night cover, and she looked very cute and tough with dark stripes drawn across her pretty white fur. Bumble looked at the coal and wasn't sure what to do or how to do it. Marguerite rolled her eyes, took the coal and painted his face for him. He felt like a child, as if his mother was cleaning his cheeks after a messy meal. Funny how many things Marguerite did that reminded him of home.

Marguerite tried to concentrate on the coal as Bumble stared at her. "So, what's the plan?" he asked. Of course Bumble already knew the plan, but he was nervous, and hearing her voice calmed his nerves.

"The Rodents and I are going in the briefcase, one of us per bomb. You, my dear, are going in Oliver's pocket. He will set one bomb inside each locomotive during his 'inspection', while you jump out and find a good spot to be a lookout for us. Each of us will hold onto our bomb as he pulls it out of the briefcase, and the magnetic plate will secure the bomb to the inside of the locomotive. Once the coast is clear, each of us will flip the switch, activate the timer and get out of the locomotive as fast as we can. Piece of cake, as you British say..."

"Well, that sounds like a winning plan to me. And it's a good thing that it's you and the Rodents going in with the bombs, since magnetism isn't my field." He waited for a response, but got none. "Hah Haaaah! Get it? Magnetism...field? *Magnetic field?*" Bumble tried to hide his concern with a bad joke. She could see right through him.

"Oh, you're cute..." she answered. "Well Dear, think of it this way. You're good at fixing things, while I'm good at blowing them up. So, between the two of us, we're the perfect pair." She smiled sweetly and kissed him. Bumble was stunned...and thrilled...and disappointed that he didn't have a chance to return the kiss. Up ahead, the rail yard came into view. Marguerite whispered, "See you soon" and climbed into the briefcase along with the Rodents. It was all starting to happen, and fast. There was no time to think. Bumble climbed into Oliver's side pocket as the car pulled up to the front gate.

Sebastian showed the guard the fake paperwork, and after a long moment the guard looked up and signaled for the gate to be opened. Thank goodness that worked. The car pulled into the train yard and Sebastian parked near the gate. He jumped out and opened the door for his senior "officer" who stood and looked around the yard with a frown. Oliver played the part of the Inspector well. He acted bored and not at all interested about being there. Out of a doorway came the train yard Superintendent, clipboard in hand. Oliver turned to face him. This should be their contact man. If he wasn't, they would be in big trouble.

From inside Oliver's pocket, Bumble could hear bits and pieces of their muffled conversation. They spoke about rain in June, flowers in a woman's hair and the toll of a bell, whatever that meant. Must have been code-speak. Now they were moving and walking in the direction of the trains. Bumble peeked out of the pocket. The train yard was enormous. Tracks crisscrossed each other in every direction, massive pieces of equipment moved slowly along the rails, and high above it all was the control tower. Maintenance men, engineers and soldiers were everywhere. They were deep in the lion's den now.

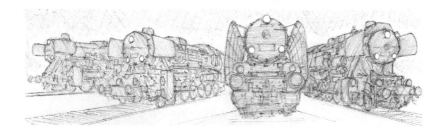

Up ahead he could see four "Class 52" locomotives waiting on their tracks. They were the largest, strongest and fastest locomotives on the German railways. The first three of them were attached to troop passenger cars, while the fourth was attached to a set of cargo flatbeds. This was the "bullet train"; the deadly weapon and supply cargo train. Bumble could see crates piled on top of crates, and rows of artillery shells that seemed to go on forever. There was even a giant tank on one of the flatbeds. His blood ran cold just seeing all of this deadly equipment in one place. How horrible man could be.

He gulped again and tried to focus on his part of the mission. He was the lookout, wasn't he? Well then, he needed to find someplace high from which to do his looking out, and in a hurry, but where?

Up ahead was a water tower, with a movable arm that swiveled into place above the passing locomotives to fill their tenders with water. The tender was the small car attached to the locomotive behind the engineer's cab; it carried water for the boiler and coal for the firebox. Every locomotive had a tender, and every locomotive needed water, so every locomotive passed under the water tower. It should give him the perfect view over all four locomotives to see exactly what was going on. Bumble jumped out of Oliver's pocket, landed on the ground and immediately started running as fast as he could.

In his black turtleneck and dark coal face paint, Bumble was almost invisible as he darted in and out of the shadows. He felt like a new mouse. Being a spy was much more exciting than cleaning tire treads, that was for sure. In the back of his mind he had a nagging worry about Marguerite in that briefcase full of bombs, but the operation was underway, and it was too late to do anything about it now.

Bumble reached the tower and started climbing. He climbed as fast as he could, and kept his eyes locked in front of him. He had to get to the top and get there quickly. Marguerite and the Rodents were counting on him. He was so focused on what he was doing, that he had forgotten about his fear of heights. He just kept climbing.

When he reached the top, he ran along the rickety water arm, all the way out to the very edge, then laid down flat, and gripped it with all of his might. He looked down. Far below, he could see Oliver and the Superintendent reach the first locomotive – the first of the three troop transport trains. Bumble tried to see who was being placed inside, but couldn't quite make it out. Oliver was doing a good job of hiding his work.

At the locomotive, the Superintendent opened the access door and pointed for the Inspector to take a look inside. Oliver pulled the first bomb out of his briefcase and placed it inside as he looked up and down the length of the boiler chamber. The bomb locked into place with a satisfying CLONG as the magnetic plate firmly attached itself to the wall. Oliver pulled out his hand and nodded his fake "approval". Inside the locomotive, Number One climbed on top of the bomb and stepped carefully over to the timer and waited. As Oliver and the Superintendent walked away, a tiny firefly buzzed into the chamber and lit up brightly so Number One could see what he was doing. Number One flipped the main switch. A small red light glowed on. The timer started ticking. The bomb was armed. Number One signaled the firefly and out they went. The firefly turned to follow Oliver and the Superintendent while Number One ran off towards the fence.

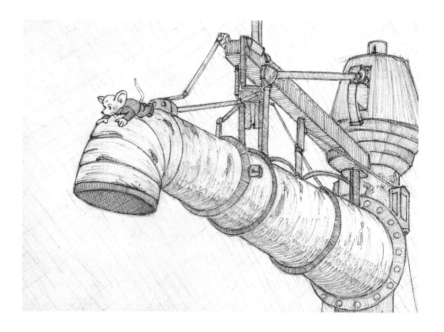

High above, Bumble saw the Rodent run out of the locomotive. As relieved as he was that the first rat was out and safe, he was disappointed that it wasn't Marguerite. Hopefully she was next.

At the second locomotive, Oliver and the Superintendent went through the same play-acting, and again the tiny firefly flew in and helped light the way for the arming of the bomb. This time it was Number Two who exited the locomotive safely.

Bumble's nose tingled. He had a terrible sinking feeling that Marguerite was going to be the last one – to arm the last bomb – in the last locomotive. The operation was halfway done. Two down, two to go. He didn't know if he could take the pressure much longer. Oliver, for his part, had started to sweat and his limbs were starting to feel like noodles from the stress.

As Oliver and the Superintendent made their way to the third locomotive, they passed the office of the train yard Commandant. The Commandant watched them pass by his window and was surprised to see an inspection at this time of night. It wasn't on his calendar, and he wondered why he hadn't been told about it. It was *his* train station after all, and he was responsible for everything that went on there. Some idiot at HQ had forgotten to tell him. It wasn't the first time. He would have to see for himself, and got up to put on his uniform jacket.

At the third locomotive, Bumble could see that all went smoothly. Number Three armed the bomb and got out and made it to the fence safely. But...that also meant Bumble was right. Marguerite was the last one. It was up to her to blow up the Bullet Train.

"Fibblejibbits..." he muttered under his breath and shook his head.

As Oliver and the Superintendent neared the fourth locomotive, Bumble saw something that almost made his heart stop. He saw the Commandant exit his office and follow them! There was no mistaking it. He was walking quickly to catch up to them. They had no idea he was coming, and probably only had seconds to plant the bomb, *if* they even got that far. Bumble froze for a moment as he watched it all play out. Then he remembered what he was there to do.

He whistled. And whistled loudly.

Oliver and the Superintendent reached the last locomotive. Behind them, they heard the Commandant call out but pretended not to hear him. They also heard Bumble's frantic whistle, and knew they were in trouble. The Superintendent quickly opened the access door while Oliver reached into his briefcase and placed the last bomb and Marguerite inside. But instead of turning to leave, they came face to face with the Commandant. He was red from yelling. Oliver did his best to look cold and disinterested, while the Superintendent was visibly terrified. The Commandant looked from one to the next, yelled again, grabbed the Superintendent's clipboard and then did the unthinkable.

He reached up and closed the access door on the locomotive.

Bumble shrieked from up on high. His heart started pounding furiously in his chest. Then, almost in slow motion, everything went terribly wrong. Oliver's nervous sweating had caused the glue on his fake bushy eyebrows to melt, and his right eyebrow fell to the ground. The Superintendent's eyes went wide when he saw this, and he panicked. He chose to save his own skin and pointed to Oliver and screamed "IMPOSTEUR!!!" Oliver dropped the empty briefcase, turned and ran. The Commandant waved to some nearby engineers, pointed to the locomotives and yelled orders for them to move the trains immediately.   He blew his whistle, while the Superintendent slipped away into the shadows and disappeared.   Oliver ran out into the open yard as a loud emergency siren started to wail and searchlights sparked to life. Then, Sebastian and the Kubelwagon came roaring in out of nowhere. Sebastian was screaming something at the top of his lungs. Looks like his temper had finally boiled over. Shots were fired.   Tires screeched, and more unseen voices yelled.   But Bumble couldn't tell what was going on because his stare was fixed on the Bullet Train.   The access door was closed, Marguerite was trapped inside, and an engineer had climbed into the cab and started the engine. He tugged on the pull chord and the Class 52's deafening whistle shrieked. Steam exploded out of the vents and the main smokestack as he put the train into gear. The giant wheels spun on the rails at first, then caught and started pulling the massive load. It chugged ahead slowly.   The Bullet Train was moving, and somehow Bumble had to stop it, or Marguerite would surely die.

22

Night Train To Nowhere

Panic. Fear. Terror. In that order. These were the thoughts that bombarded Bumble's brain as the Bullet Train started to pull out onto the tracks directly below him. What on earth could he do from so high up on the water tower? How could he possibly help her in time? Then...one after another...the timers on the bombs...timed out.

The first locomotive exploded.

Then came the second.

Then the third.

One enormous explosion after another.

BOOM!

KA-BOOM!

KA-BLAAM!

Blinding flashes of red and orange fire lit up the train yard. For Bumble's sensitive ears, the sound was thunderous, unbearable and deafening. The ground shook like an earthquake. Massive hunks of twisted metal went flying everywhere.

A shockwave knocked Bumble right off of the tower. He caught the edge and tried to hold on, dangling over the tracks, first with both of his hands, then one, then just a few fingers, then none. He lost his grip and cartwheeled through the air, falling toward certain doom. He closed his eyes. This was the end. There was nothing left to do but accept his final moments quietly and respectfully, like a proper gentleman.

"WAAAAAAHHHHHH!" he screamed all the way down.

And then, to his surprise, he splashed into ice-cold water, and everything went silent. He drifted down for a long moment, submerged in the deep and cold black water. What was this? Was he dead? Was this Heaven? After a few seconds, he kicked up to the surface, opened his eyes and saw that he was still very much alive, floating in the railcar tender behind the engineer's compartment. Water for the boiler, coal for the firebox, of course! One fraction of a second earlier or later, and he would have been one dead-splat mouse. He looked up to the sky.

"Thank you," he said from the bottom of his heart. The endless blanket of stars winked back at him.

Bumble was now on the Bullet Train. As it picked up speed and screamed out of the station into the darkness, he thought of Marguerite, and climbed out of the water compartment with renewed energy, strength and purpose. They were both going to come out of this alive, and he would give his last breath and the very last beat of his heart to do it. But just *how* he would do it, he had no idea. This locomotive was no airplane, but it *was* a machine, and machines were his specialty. Time to get moving.

The three explosions meanwhile could be seen and heard for miles. Which was a very good thing, because now that it had gotten dark, Robin Winchester was beginning to think she would never find Bumble or his Resistance pals. She had been flying for hours up and down every waterway looking for the Floating Fortress of whatever it was called, but she could not find it. Wherever Bumble was, she was certain he would be in the middle of the action.

"Follow the explosions..." was the advice Dudley had given her, and it turns out he was right. In the distance she saw the three fireballs light up the night sky. It was just the lucky break she needed. In no time, she flew over the train yard and landed on top of Bumble's water tower to get a better look at what was going on. Fire crews were running everywhere, frantically trying to put out the fires on the three exploded locomotives. Two officers pointed down the empty tracks into the distance while motorcycles drove out of the main gate to chase after another vehicle. From the looks of things, Bumble and his Resistance pals had come here to blow up some trains. Well, check that off the list. Now, what to do next? Robin could either fly south and follow the motorcycles, or fly east and follow the train tracks, but which? If she made the wrong choice, she may never get a second chance at finding Bumble. But she knew exactly what to do.

Robin swooped down from the water tower and followed the empty tracks into the darkness.

Inside the locomotive, it was hot. It was dark. And it was incredibly loud. Marguerite pulled frantically on the access door handle, but it wouldn't budge. The firefly's light started to dim as he buzzed every which way, trying to find a way out. They were sealed in. As the locomotive picked up speed, it only got louder and hotter.

Marguerite tried her best to stay calm and think clearly, but she knew they wouldn't survive in here for very long. She cupped her hands to her mouth and called out as loudly as she could:

"HELP! SOMEBODY HELP! WE'RE TRAPPED IN HERE!"

Her voice just echoed back against the thundering boom of the engine. There was no chance that anyone on the outside could have heard her. She could hardly hear her own echo.

Marguerite felt her energy drain. She pulled on the door latch one last time with all of her might. Nothing. Her hands started to shake, and she slumped down next to the bomb. She looked at the timer and considered whether or not to just go ahead and start it. If she was going to go, why not take the locomotive with her and at least complete the mission. She thought long and hard about what to do. And in that moment, in her mind's eye, all she could see was Bumble. Sweet, gentle Bumble Humblestone, who loved her cooking and treated her like a lady, who was kind and generous and thoughtful. If she set the bomb off, that meant she would have to let him go, and she wasn't prepared to do that.

Her panic turned to sadness. If this *was* the end, she had never gotten the chance to tell him how she really felt. She buried her face in her hands. Everything around her was shaking and banging. Her ears started to ring, and the poor firefly flickered on and off. Soon Marguerite wouldn't be able to see or hear anything. It looked as though she was going to die in here and die alone.

"BUMBLE!" she cried out.

She listened for his reply, hoping against hope for a response, but heard nothing. After that, there was only hot loud darkness.

Bumble meanwhile made his way to the engineer's compartment. His thinking was sharp and clear. Underneath the locomotive it was all spinning wheels and moving parts –

way too dangerous to try to get in that way. The engineer's compartment held the firebox, which led to the interior chamber, but he'd burn to a crisp if he tried that. The smokestack wasn't a realistic way in either – he'd choke from the smoke. That left only the front of the train as a possible way in.

He snuck past the engineer, climbed down to the running board and ran as fast as he could down the length of the locomotive. When he got to the access panel door he climbed up and pulled on the handle, but it didn't budge. No surprise. He kept running.

At the front of the locomotive the oncoming wind slapped him hard in the face and almost knocked him over. They had to be moving at close to full speed, and the tracks below whizzed by at a dizzying pace. It reminded him of being on *Eightball Charlie*'s landing gear during takeoff, but with one big difference. This time, he wasn't afraid. He had to save Marguerite.

He studied the face of the locomotive and climbed down onto the coupler near the tracks to get a better look. At first, there didn't seem to be any clear way in, just rivets and bolts and iron. But Class 52 locomotives had three very large headlamps on their face: one on the lower left, one on the lower right and one high in the center towards the top. And the light bulb in the center one was broken. That was his way in!

"Ha! Victory!"

He pulled out a small rock stuck in the framing, gripped it between his teeth and climbed up the face, grabbing the rivets and bolts and using them as footholds, like a mountain climber. Again, he remembered climbing up the cockpit instruments of *Eightball Charlie* in much the same way. He got to the top as quickly as he could. There, in the center light fixture, the big broken bulb sat waiting. A small wedge of glass had broken off, like a slice removed from an apple pie, and it was just enough to give him a head start.

Bumble lifted the rock, closed his eyes and started smashing the bulb with all of his might. Glass flew everywhere in the wind. It cut his arm and stung his face, but he kept bashing until all of the glass was gone and only the stump of the metal base remained in the socket. He dropped the rock, grabbed the base and tried to push it counterclockwise.

"Righty-tighty, lefty-loosey!" he yelled.

At first, nothing happened. Bumble was furious. The clock was ticking.

"Come on! You stupid thing!"

He gritted his teeth, made the meanest face he knew and tried again.

"Turn!"

This time it budged a little bit. Then it started to move. The sharp edge of the base cut his hands as he turned it, but the threads of the bulb slowly inched out of the socket. He groaned and kept turning and turning until, finally, the base came all the way out of the socket. He let it drop and it blew away in a flash.

Bumble looked inside the empty socket and found a space that was more than big enough for him to squeeze in. He rubbed his tired bleeding hands, took a deep breath and climbed into the darkness of the main chamber.

Inside it was loud, hot and pitch black. Arms outstretched, he slowly felt his way along the left side where he knew the access door and bomb were eventually supposed to be. As his eyes adjusted, he thought he could make out a tiny speck of dim light up ahead. It was the firefly! He cupped his hands to his mouth.

"HELLO?!"

No response. He kept inching forward and tried again.

"ARE THERE ANY BEAUTIFUL MICE ON THE TRAIN?"

The tiny speck of light grew slightly brighter.

"IF SO, WOULD YOU PLEASE COME WITH ME..."

The light grew stronger.

"NO TICKET, NO RIDE. SORRY, BUT THOSE ARE THE RULES..."

The light shot up and buzzed over to meet him. The firefly glowed brightly and circled Bumble in a victory lap. Around and around it buzzed.

"Yes hello, happy to see you too!" Bumble said to the firefly. "Now, shed some light on the situation, would you?"

The firefly lit up as brightly as it could and led the way. After a few more feet Marguerite finally became visible. She was lying face down. Bumble turned her over very gently. She looked like a terrible mess, but she was still breathing. Bumble never felt so relieved in his life.

He gently shook her, and her eyes fluttered open.

"Good morning!" he said.

Her eyes went wide with relief. She grabbed his neck and squeezed him tight.

"You came back for me..." she whispered.

"I love to travel by train this time of year." He tried to mask his relief with a joke, but there were tears in his eyes. She sat up weakly and looked around. The access door above them was still closed.

"How are we going to get out of here?" she asked.

"Together."

She hugged him again.

"Can you walk?" he asked gently.

"Yes of course...don't be...silly." She tried to get up but her legs wobbled and she became dizzy with the effort. "Just give me a minute..." As she sat back down, Bumble tried to open the access door. No luck. He looked over at the bomb and timer.

"Speaking of a minute, how do I start this thing? You being an expert at blowing things up and all that." He winked. She pointed to the timer. It looked like a stopwatch. Curly wires connected it to the detonator, which was screwed onto a block of plastic explosive with a small brass cap. He sniffed the explosive.

"Now it smells like toasted almonds!" he said excitedly. His stomach rumbled in reply. But Marguerite was serious. This was no time to fool around.

"Bumble, pay attention. You are going to have to activate the bomb." He was surprised, and it took a moment to sink in. She continued. "On the face of the timer you will see two dials: the big outer dial and a smaller dial just above the center of the timepiece. The outer dial counts seconds, while the inner dial counts minutes. Take a look at the small dial and tell me what you see."

Bumble climbed up onto the bomb. The firefly buzzed over to help him see.

"Looks like five minutes."

Marguerite frowned. It wasn't enough time.

"Five minutes!" she said.

"Is it a problem?"

"Five minutes would have been plenty of time to get clear of the explosion – *if* we were still in the train yard, not moving, with an open access door. But we *are* moving, we're

194

locked in, it's pitch black and I'm very weak – so all things considered, it's not looking good."

"'Not looking good' is what I'm known for!" Bumble said with a wink as he reached over and pressed the starter button on the timer. CLICK! The second hand started to chip-chip-chip across the outer ring. The red light turned on. The bomb was activated. Five minutes to KA-BOOM. There was no turning back now. Marguerite's eyes went wide. She wasn't ready.

"What! Just how are we going to get out of here?!" she asked in alarm.

"Like I said, *together*."

Bumble jumped down, scooped Marguerite up in his arms and started running towards the front of the train with all of his might. The firefly flew out in front of them and led the way while Marguerite held on tightly.

As they ran, Marguerite could feel the cool night air rushing in from up ahead. It was the sweetest air she had ever tasted. She smiled and breathed deeply as they reached the front. Bumble set her down and pointed to the gap behind the light bulb socket. Through the gap she could see the dark outline of trees zooming by.

"You'll have to squeeze through this. When you get through, stay put – and watch out for broken glass. Got it?" She nodded her head 'yes'. "Now, out you go!"

Marguerite eased through the gap to the outside. The wind whipped her around and she grabbed the sides of the light socket to keep steady. Against all hope or reason, here she was, alive. She could hardly believe it. She was out. Her teeth started to chatter as she shivered uncontrollably. It had to be thirty degrees colder outside, maybe more. Not that she was complaining. She had never been more grateful to see the stars. They twinkled back, just like they did for Bumble.

Bumble eased out of the gap and the firefly followed. The little guy got blown around violently at first, but after a moment, he started to hover and glow brightly. Bumble turned to Marguerite.

"Hello," he said.

"Hello," she answered.

"Can you walk?"

"I can walk, but I think we're going to have to run..." Marguerite was getting a second wind. Bumble nodded his head in agreement.

Four minutes to explosion.

23

The Clock Runs Out

"Okay, follow me. Up and over."

Bumble climbed up and over the light fixture and reached down for Marguerite's hand. He pulled her up and in no time they were on the top of the locomotive. The firefly sped out in front of them and they started running down the length towards the engineer's station. The rushing wind at their backs helped push them along, and they covered the distance very quickly.

The train engineer, meanwhile, was alone on the train. The Commandant had ordered him to get the train out of the station as quickly as possible, and in all the panic – without really thinking – he did just as he was ordered, and didn't wait for guards, soldiers or anyone else to join him. He was to drive the train to the next station and wait for further orders. It was a station over twenty-five miles away, on the other side of the river, and from what he remembered, it had very good food, so he was looking very forward to arriving there. He secretly hoped he could stay the night and get some sleep as well. His bunkmate snored something awful, and he just wanted some peace.

As he strained his eyes and looked ahead into the murky darkness, he thought he saw two little mice running along the top of the locomotive following, of all things, a firefly. That was funny. His mind must be playing tricks on him. He remembered the time he thought he saw a fierce bird of prey pecking and scratching at the base of the smokestack, when all it turned out to be was a dirty maintenance rag blowing in the wind. These "mice" were probably just a few leaves blowing around on the train. Sometimes the darkness and moving shadows played tricks on him. He shook his head, blinked and looked again. Nothing. Certainly, a good hot dinner would help to clear his head.

He yawned loudly and stretched. And when he opened his eyes, the firefly was hovering right in front of him. It buzzed brightly and circled his head. The engineer swatted at it and missed. It flew down to the floor and lit up the two mice he didn't think he saw before. They play-acted a show. It was funny and sweet and strange.

The first mouse pointed to the front of the locomotive and spread its fingers out like a flower, while the other one drew a finger across its neck, closed its eyes and stuck out its tongue. The first one then pointed urgently to its wrist like there was a watch there, and the other one ran in place and pointed to the back of the train. This was really adorable, but he had no idea what they were trying to say. Was he supposed to deliver flowers to the station up ahead at a specific time and was running late and was therefore dead meat? The mice each slapped their foreheads in frustration.

"He doesn't understand!" Marguerite cried. "This poor idiot is going to die. After all, he only drives the train. He doesn't deserve to die. What can we do?"

"I'll take care of him...go!" Bumble motioned for Marguerite to start running, and she took off.

Bumble ran over to the engineer and started tugging on the cuff of his pants and pointing towards the back of the train. The engineer looked down and smiled. Bumble then pulled on the man's shoelace, but it only untied. This was going nowhere. There wasn't any time to fool around! That bomb was ticking. So, Bumble decided to do something he never dared to do before. He climbed up the engineer's shoe, pulled down his sock and bit his leg. It was more of a nibble really, but it didn't matter. The engineer shouted, his face turned red and his eyes went wide in anger. He started stomping his feet down on the compartment floor planks, trying to squash little Bumble.

"No good deed goes unpunished in this war!" Bumble said to no one in particular. The engineer's shoe slammed directly behind him, and clipped the end of his tail.

"Whoa! Fibblejibbits! Fibblejibbits!" Bumble started running. He now had second thoughts about saving this doofus, but what was done was done. Add one furious engineer to the ticking time bomb on the runaway equipment train racing through enemy territory in the dead of night. In less than four minutes it would all be over, one way or another.

As Bumble ran across the top of the coals on the tender and passed the narrow water compartment, he could see Marguerite already climbing onto the next car. He got splashed from coals ker-plunking into the water as the engineer pitched his best throws at him.

"When I get back to England, no more planes, no more trains, no more running, jumping or falling down! I'm going to find something nice and quiet to do, and find somewhere nice and quiet to do it…smoke a pipe…play some chess! Eat some cheese! That sounds like a good plan, right?!" Three minutes and counting.

Bumble ran the obstacle course of the second car. It was an enormous flatbed covered with a maze of wooden crates and row after row of artillery shells. Everything was carefully tied down for transport, but that didn't make it any less dangerous. The crates were jammed full with ammunition, rifles, pistols, and grenades, while the artillery shells came in two sizes: huge and enormous. Bumble weaved in and out and made it to the end of the car in no time. The engineer meanwhile was trying to force one of the crates open. What would he find inside? How would he use it? Maybe it was best not to think about it.

Marguerite was waiting for Bumble at the beginning of the next car. It was another flatbed, but this one carried a gigantic Panzer Tank and two Howitzer Artillery Guns, more machines of death. She grabbed his hand. "Not much time left!" she yelled, and they ran together with the firefly leading the way.

Two minutes to go.

As they ran along the side of the tank Bumble was amazed at how strong and yet how delicate the complicated treads appeared to be. Marguerite pulled him along. No time to play mechanic now. Ahead, thankfully, was the end of the flatbed. They climbed down and across the coupler to the next and final flatbed. This one, to their great relief, was empty. Its wide and long expanse of empty planks was a welcome sight.

One minute until detonation.

"Almost there!" Marguerite yelled. They sprinted across the empty space in a matter of seconds. At the far end they looked down to see the tracks zooming fast below them. Without the engineer at the controls, the train had gradually picked up speed on its own. They looked to the left and to the right, only to see the dense dark forest whizzing by close to the tracks, too close unfortunately. There was nowhere left to go and there were only seconds left.

"Looks like the end...sorry sweetness, guess I didn't really plan it out too well, did I?" Bumble said regretfully.

His mind was scrambling to figure a way off the train that didn't involve immediate death. They were simply going too fast and there was nowhere safe to jump. He took her hand in his and squeezed it tightly. She smiled warmly and pulled him into a hug.

"You came back for me. Which is more than anyone else I know would have ever done. No matter what happens, I want you to know that. Thank you." Bumble smiled and squeezed her tight.

And then, as if on cue, they heard a crazy laugh behind them as the engineer climbed up onto the platform, holding of all things, a shovel, pulled from one of the crates. Bumble could hardly believe it. The engineer lifted it like an ax, swung it through the air and banged it down on the planking. WHAAANG!

"We're moments from death and he's still playing games?" Bumble was beside himself. He stepped out in front of Marguerite to protect her from the engineer and put up his fists. She leaned in and yelled over his shoulder.

"Well Darling, if we blow up, we blow up together…"

"NOT TODAY!" yelled a voice from behind.

Bumble and Marguerite turned to see a beautiful white bird swoop down out of the darkness. It was Robin Winchester! She angled her wings, flew straight into the headwind, and gently drifted into position just above them. She eased her talons down to within easy reach. Bumble couldn't believe it.

"Grab on!" she screamed.

Marguerite looked to Bumble who nodded 'yes, do it!' and they both reached up and grabbed a leg. Robin pulled them up and off of the platform with ease. As the train sped away, the engineer dropped his shovel in disappointment. He had really wanted to smash that little mouse. Behind him, the tracks turned onto a long bridge over a river and the locomotive started to make its way across.

Very gently, Robin set Bumble and Marguerite down a few feet away from the tracks, and immediately, everyone collapsed in exhaustion. What a relief it was to not be moving anymore.

"Solid ground never felt so good!" Bumble said happily.

"Oh, I agree!" Marguerite excitedly replied. They all laughed, sighed deeply and laughed some more. They were safe.

Then, deep inside the locomotive of the Bullet Train, the igniter sent a charge into the plastic explosive and it detonated.

The explosion was tremendous.

Already midway across the bridge, the locomotive jumped the tracks. It smashed into the support beams on the right side, snapped them like toothpicks and came to rest halfway off the bridge, dangling over open space. Its enormous wheels continued spinning and as the locomotive's weight settled, they started grinding and pounding into the thick stone and concrete, sending clouds of powdery debris down to the river below. Pieces of superheated metal flew in all directions, and hot fragments hit the ammunition crates and artillery shells on the second car. Belts of ammunition started firing off like firecrackers on the Fourth of July, and bullets shot through the crates and into row after row of neatly tied down artillery shells. The shells started igniting and a series of chain reaction explosions followed, one bigger than the next. In moments, the middle of the bridge was completely blown away, and everything fell into the river. Every last bit of everything.

The locomotive hissed loudly as it was swallowed up by the bubbling steaming river, the tank and guns disappeared quickly below the surface, and the useless bridge above was now left without a middle section and burning at either end. The engineer popped up out of the water, shook his fist, yelled something in German as he was quickly carried away downstream.

Bumble, Marguerite and Robin watched it all, amazed. It was probably the most spectacular thing any of them had ever seen.

"Well *there's* something you don't see every day!" said Robin, impressed. Bumble leaned over to Marguerite.

"And you said I was only good at fixing things," he said proudly.

"I stand corrected..." she answered, equally proud and impressed.

After another moment of stunned silence, Robin smiled and looked at Bumble. "You! You're quite a hard mouse to find Mister Bumble Humblestone!" she said.

Marguerite was surprised. She pointed to Robin.

"You know her? She knows you?"

"Yes, we know each other..." Robin replied mysteriously.

Bumble was oblivious to the strong hint of jealousy coming from Marguerite. Robin saw through it and laughed.

"Oh no Dearie, it's nothing like that. Mister Bumble here gave me some important navigation coordinates to transport to the Resistance earlier this week. Seems like a long time ago, doesn't it Bumble?"

"It sure does." Bumble answered. "What a difference a day makes." He smiled at Marguerite. Robin stuck out her wing for an introduction.

"Robin Winchester, Confidential Pigeon Service, at your service Madam."

Marguerite relaxed and offered her hand.

"Marguerite LaFleur, French Underground, at yours." They shook hands and wings happily.

"Oh! So the coordinates were for you!" Robin said.

"Yes, ultimately I suppose they were."

"And everything worked out I hope?"

Marguerite looked to Bumble and smiled. "Oh yes, everything worked out." Robin decided not to break the mood. These mice had been through a lot. She had better get going.

"Very well then. I will report back to you here at daybreak, and fly you wherever you wish to go. So please don't go wandering off. This is our spot. Here. Daybreak. Agreed?"

"Agreed," Bumble and Marguerite replied.

"See you in a few hours. Enjoy the fire." Robin nodded at the bridge, winked and then flew up and away. Bumble and Marguerite watched her disappear into the night sky. A thick blanket of stars sparkled as far as the eye could see. Marguerite sighed deeply – and happily – and laid back down.

Bumble meanwhile stood up and looked around to try to get an idea of where they were, and noticed two things. The first was a sign above them pointing in the direction of what was left of the bridge that read: *"Le Pont de Port-Bail"* ("The Port-Bail Bridge"). The second was that Robin had dropped them in a bed of flowers, daisies to be exact. She may not have known what it meant, but Bumble sure did. He pulled a loose daisy off the ground and showed it to Marguerite with a big smile.

"What are the chances of that?" he asked.

"Chances of what?" Marguerite answered.

"This flower! The Daisy. It was originally called the 'Day's Eye' because it looks like the brilliant daytime sun. Over time, 'day's eye' turned into 'daisy', and for us, it's a nickname for girls with a sunny disposition named Margaret. So, in England, your nickname would be Daisy. Which is what we're sitting in, and surrounded by. Isn't that something?" Bumble was quite excited to have figured that out.

"You can call me that." Marguerite said.

"What? Daisy?"

"Yes please. From now on."

"Oh, alright then, Daisy it is. Hello Daisy."

"Hello Bumble, pleased to meet you."

They both smiled. This was another major twist to the day. Daisy was touched and worked up the courage to ask him something that was on her mind.

"Bumble?"

"Yes Daisy?" He liked the sound of her new name.

"When Robin comes back, what are we going to tell her? I mean about where to take us?" Daisy's eyes were suddenly very big and moist. She continued, "There's nothing left for me here now. The team is scattered. Now that the mission is done, I'm done." Bumble could see she meant every word.

"Until I met you, I was just a nobody, going nowhere, living a nothing life" said Bumble.

"You could never be nobody to me..." she said sweetly and hugged him tight. He offered her the daisy.

"I want you to come to England with me. Would that be alright?" She hoped he would feel this way, as this is what she was thinking as well. She nodded and relaxed in his arms.

"Yes, I suppose I could lay low...come to England for a while..."

"One more thing..." he said. "I probably should have mentioned this before, but Bumble is just a silly nickname I've had for a long time. My real name is Henry."

"Henry! Oh, I like that. Henry Humblestone. Nice to meet you, Henry Humblestone." Daisy squeezed him again.

"But Henry, Bumble isn't so silly you know, it's very sweet..." she added.

"Well, you can call me whatever you like."

"And so I will, Monsieur Whatever-You-Like," she teased.

They rested there for the remainder of the night, looked at the stars and eventually drifted off into a deep sleep. Bumble enjoyed a very long and very happy dream of flying Daisy in a biplane model over fields of daisies in the bright daytime sun.

24

Reunion, Relief... And Revelation

"**W**akey wakey!"

Bumble's eyes fluttered open to see Daisy, Robin and an older scruffy bird he didn't know looking down at him. Daisy was all smiles.

"Time to go home..." she said.

"Before something else happens!" Robin added.

Bumble sat up and rubbed his neck. He was sore from yesterday's action, and the day before that, and the day before *that*. Sore from the top of his ears to the tip of his tail. He yawned loudly and turned to see the sun peeking up from the horizon. It was daybreak all right, the crack of dawn, just like Robin promised. Bumble wished he could have rested just a little while longer, like maybe another 20 hours. The older bird took a step forward.

"You're not afraid of heights, are you?" he asked. The question caught Bumble off guard.

"I used to be – wait – why?" he answered suspiciously.

The old bird leaned in close, squinted one eye closed and said, "Do you really want to know?" Bumble decided that he really didn't want to know and left it alone. He yawned again.

"Bumble, this is Wally. Wally Winchester. My Dad." Robin said proudly. Wally stuck out his wing, and gave Bumble a handshake that almost lifted him up off the ground.

"Stand tall little mouse! From what I hear, you did big things here in France. So, let's get you back home to England in one piece, shall we? You'll be flying with me." Bumble nodded, put up his hand and raised one finger.

"Yes, but before we go, is there anything to eat? Or even just some water to drink?" he asked. Wally squinted at Bumble again.

"Water? That stuff rusts pipes and sinks ships! And you want to drink it?" he said. Bumble was too tired to tell if he was kidding or serious, and just looked at him blankly. Wally laughed and handed over a small canteen from his supply pouch and Bumble drank gratefully. Daisy meanwhile climbed up on Robin's back, grabbed hold of her collar and was eager to get started.

"All set!" Daisy called out.

"Up you go!" Robin said to Bumble, and pointed to Wally's back.

Bumble nodded tiredly and Wally eased his wing down to help Bumble climb up. "Watch the feathers, Mate" Wally said. Bumble straddled Wally's shoulders and grabbed hold of his collar. Wally shrugged, centered Bumble's weight, straightened back up and crouched into take-off position.

"You ready?" Wally asked.

"You really want to know?" Bumble answered.

"Ha! You're funny! Here goes nothing – we touch down in a few hours!"

And with that, Robin and Wally Winchester launched into the sky, and headed due north. It was a calm and beautiful morning, and Daisy was filled with absolute joy. She felt the wind in her fur, breathed the crisp morning air and enjoyed a view of the sunrise she had only dreamed of. It was heaven.

For Robin, it was rare to have someone along to talk to, other than herself, and so she and Daisy chatted the whole way very happily. They talked about Bumble of course, and of how sweet and courageous he was. Daisy related the whole locomotive ordeal in detail and Robin was very horrified and impressed.

Wally talked a good deal as well, but Bumble only heard little bits here and there, as he fought very hard to stay awake. He heard something about Wally's love of beer, his dislike of fish of any sort (after all, they live in the water and water is dangerous stuff), his taste for strong mustard on everything and the wisdom of surrender when it comes to females, as they can neither be lived with nor lived without, whatever that meant. Bumble eventually drifted off to sleep, slouched against Wally's neck and started to snore loudly. Wally guessed the little mouse wasn't afraid of heights anymore, and that was a very good thing.

The four of them flew peacefully north over occupied France and across the English Channel without incident. Robin was especially thankful, as she never wanted to get involved in a dogfight ever again. They reached the coast in record time and eventually found their way up to Station 102 of Air Transport Command.

Things at the base had gotten busy and relatively back to normal, with lots of cargo coming and going on a very tight schedule. A further investigation of Davenport's quarters had turned up a secret radio in his footlocker, a small German code book and "Deutsche Reichsbank" ("Central Bank of Germany") papers equal to ten thousand dollars made out in his name. Of course, everyone thought about the failure of the big mission, but no one really wanted to talk about it. It was the blackest of black eyes for Station 102. The shock of betrayal, the disappointment of loss, and the feeling of being duped were all fresh in everyone's minds and they all stung badly.

It was especially heartbreaking for those unfortunate three who were most directly affected – Crash, Archie and Chief. Each in his own way felt a heavy responsibility for what had happened.

The mission review meeting was scheduled for twelve noon, and Commander Hammond had requested everyone at the base to attend. Officials from London had also invited themselves at the last minute, which made it even worse. Public humiliation was certain, and a demotion or dishonorable discharge might not be very far behind. It was like waiting for an execution. No doubt the base would soon close, and everyone would be reassigned elsewhere. Today had the makings of a very sad day.

A few minutes before noon, two carrier pigeons appeared in the sky over the base. Chief was the first to notice, and as he sniffed the air he caught a familiar scent. He sniffed again to make sure, and there was no mistake – it was Bumble! Chief started barking loudly as the birds approached, and he exploded into several circular victory laps around them as they gently touched down. Bumble woke to the sound of his friend's barking and had never heard a more welcome sound. He could hardly believe his eyes, and was beside himself to not only be back at the base, but to see his loyal best friend. He jumped off of Wally's back and ran to meet Chief who gave him a big wet lick and a tight loving hug. Both friends shed a tear of happiness.

"I thought you were lost!" Chief said.

"I almost was, old friend." Bumble voice cracked with emotion. He motioned to Daisy who came over, and Chief's eyes went wide. Daisy hugged Bumble tight.

"Daisy, meet the best friend a mouse ever had – the one and only Chief. Old buddy, this is Daisy."

"Hello Chief." Daisy smiled.

At first, Chief was at a loss for words. This was almost too much for one dog to take. Not only was Bumble back, but he was back with a lady friend. And one so pretty! It must have been a busy couple of days. Chief decided he would have to wait to get the full story from Bumble. After all, they had a mission review to get to. He tried his best to be proper.

"Welcome to Station 102, lovely lady. I sure am happy to meet you."

"As am I." Daisy smiled again.

"You're just in time for our sentencing," Chief said as cheerfully as he could, and smiled a sad ironic smile. "And to hear when they are going to close the base."

"What?!" Bumble exclaimed.

"Yep – starting now – can't be late. Time to learn our fates. Pay the piper. Cook our goose and all that."

Chief started walking towards the Briefing Room, head hung low. Bumble and Daisy turned to Robin and Wally. It was time to say goodbye.

"Thank you, Miss Robin. And thank you too, Mister Wally. We owe you one, getting us out of trouble and getting us home safely," Bumble said.

"Bah! Think nothing of it!" Wally exclaimed.

"All part of Confidential Pigeon Service protocol. We fly. We fight. We triumph." Robin answered confidently.

"Until next time." Daisy said and squeezed Robin's wing. Robin smiled a reassuring smile and winked.

"We'll meet again. Of that you can be certain." She turned to her father. "Come on Pop! No dilly-dallying! Time to go!"

Wally nodded in agreement. "Very well then." He pointed at Bumble. "You stand tall little mouse! Remember –

214

stay away from water – that's nasty stuff…" And with that, father and daughter took off into the bright blue sky. Bumble realized it was the third time he had watched her fly away into the distance. It probably wouldn't be the last.

Once they disappeared, Bumble and Daisy followed Chief into the Briefing Room. As the clock struck twelve, an official looking vehicle approached, and two figures exited. Bumble marveled at how precise the military could be.

Inside, everyone was already seated and waiting. Crash, Archie and Chief had been asked to sit in the front row. They looked like death warmed over, had lumps in their throats from nerves and their breathing was shallow from anxiety. Bumble and Daisy made their way up front and sat next to Chief to show their support. Crash and Archie just stared ahead, lost in their thoughts. The room quieted down as Hammond walked to the front. He cleared his throat. Here it comes.

"Congratulations Gentlemen, Operation Mercury was a tremendous success!"

At first, no one understood. What was he saying? He continued. "We've suspected that all the recent accidents at Station 102 couldn't have *all* been accidents. They had to be the work of someone working behind the scenes, in secret. So, together with Headquarters, we invented the elaborate communications package as a decoy to smoke him out. And it worked. Davenport revealed himself to be the saboteur and he spoiled the mission in spectacular fashion. Wouldn't you men agree?" He looked at Crash and Archie, who could only nod back in awed shock. What was happening? Hammond continued. "But the good news is, you men *did* manage to drop the secondary cargo – the standard supply canister – right

215

where you were supposed to. And that's where things get interesting. Gentlemen, if you please..."

Hammond motioned to the back of the room and the two officials from London made their way to the front to join him. The first official carried a briefcase handcuffed to his wrist while the other carried a folded-up artist's easel. Archie almost fell out of his chair when he saw them. It was Agents Picadilly and Pointblank (today's codenames) from The Cabinet War Rooms! As they set up the easel and undid the handcuffs, Picadilly spoke first.

"We were given the job of inventing a communications device for the French Resistance that could be easily delivered and would avoid detection when used. Their mail is routinely intercepted, and their telephones are tapped. So, how to get them to correspond in a way that guaranteed them that what they were receiving was an authentic message from another Resistance member and not something from the enemy?"

Pointblank continued. "This is supposedly where the Top-Secret Communications Device came in. An elaborate, beautifully crafted state-of-the-art piece of machinery. Part telephone, part radio, part typewriter – and all junk!"

The crowd gasped.

"They'll spend a month trying to figure out how to get it to work, and it won't. It's rubbish. Mechanical odds and ends that we had lying around the workshop thrown together into something impressive looking."

Picadilly pulled a small radio receiver box out of the briefcase and held it up for everyone to see. "Well, to be honest, it does do *one* thing. It allows us to listen in whenever the main unit is turned on." He turned the volume on the receiver up, and through the small speaker everyone could hear faint scratchy German. The voice on the other end did not sound happy. "They've brought it all the way to Berlin and have had several frustrated teams of people trying to figure out how it works. Rumor has it the Führer himself may now want to see it. If we knew that, we would have planted a bomb on the thing. Oh, and from what we can tell, your friend Davenport has been arrested for bringing them something that doesn't work."

The assembly broke into spontaneous applause. Amazing! Crash and Archie looked at each other in disbelief. Chief barked loudly in approval. They were saved. The mood in the room changed in an instant. But the good news wasn't over yet.

Pointblank continued. "So, if the mission wasn't about the Top-Secret machine, what was it about?" He paused dramatically. "Well, I'll tell you." He pulled out two large demonstration cards and set them side by side on the artist's easel.

"It was about stamps!"

Now it was Bumble's turn to be amazed. Daisy's eyes went wide in surprise too. Pointblank pointed to the two cards – each had a large photographic blowup of a French stamp featuring Mercury holding a flaming torch. It was the exact type of stamp the Agents had dropped into the supply canister moments before it was sealed, that Bumble had saved from getting wet on the Minkies, and that Daisy had then handed out to the other Resistance members before the mission.

Pointblank used a pointer to illustrate. "One of these is real, and one them is fake. Take a close look. What do you see? On first glance these stamps are identical. The text is the same. Mercury is in the same position. The coloring is the same. But notice that on this one…" – he pointed to the one on the right – "…Mercury is winking, and the flames of the torch are blowing in the opposite direction. Plus, here's something the Germans would never see. This is my favorite part." He ran the pointer along the paper perforations around the outside of the stamp. "The authentic stamp has thirteen and a half perforations along the top and bottom and fourteen along the sides, while the forged stamp has eleven and a half top and bottom by eleven and a half on the sides." Everyone was stunned. You could hear a pin drop.

Picadilly brought it to a close. "So in conclusion, how do you easily arm the Resistance with a communications device that will guarantee them authentic messaging between members? You do it with a stamp that only the Resistance would be in possession of. When they receive an envelope with the new forged stamp, they'll know it's from one of their own members. If they receive an envelope with the regular old stamp, they'll know it's a sneaky German message. All they have to do is look for the tell-tale markers and they'll know instantly what they've got. It's simple, it's inexpensive and it's very effective. The design has been passed on for additional printing." He looked down at Bumble and Daisy. "Sometimes the smallest things can make the biggest difference."

Pointblank got in the last word, "We specialize in the unconventional, the irregular and the unexpected, and we are quite proud to do so. Thanks to you, the stamps are now in Resistance circulation. Well done Station 102!"

The room again erupted into shouts, hoots and whistles of every kind. All the men threw their hats into the air. Bumble and Daisy hugged each other. Crash and Archie shook hands and laughed in relief. Hammond applauded for the Agents, and the Agents applauded for everyone in the assembly. Station 102 pulled off a double mission and they didn't even know it. In seemingly endless days of war, this was a rare day of triumph. Only Inspector Baxter seemed displeased, as he found all of the celebration distasteful. He frowned, shook his head and left the Briefing Room, alone.

Chief scooped Bumble and Daisy up and ran a victory lap around the room, barking and howling all the way. Crash and Archie expressed their great relief to Hammond, and the Agents congratulated Archie on the part he played. Even Smiley Reilly smiled and shook Victor Wisniewski's hand.

When Chief circled back around, Crash petted him happily and saw Bumble and Daisy for the first time. He was surprised, thrilled and relieved. Could this day get any better?

"Good Heavens! Bumble! You're alive! Welcome back!" he said and turned to Archie. "Look who's here!" Archie couldn't believe his eyes.

"Hey! It's you! Wait a minute, I have something for you." He reached into his pocket and pulled out Bumble's tiny shovel. "I believe this is yours…" he said as he crouched down and handed it to Bumble. "Terribly sorry about dropping you out of the plane and all of that…"

"Best thing that ever happened to me." Bumble turned to Daisy and gave her a wink. He showed her the shovel. "We could have used this last night." Daisy agreed. "Hmm-hmmm. Oh well…"

Happily reunited with his trusty shovel, Bumble hefted it in his hands and thought of how much things had changed, and shook his head in amazement. Things certainly had changed. Then, out of the corner of his eye and through the crowd, he caught a glimpse of Ed and Fred. How incredibly fitting. They waved 'hello' and took a step in Bumble's direction, but then stopped, awkwardly. It was clear they didn't know what to do, so Bumble walked over to shake their hands and show there were no hard feelings.

Crash bent down to speak to Daisy. He pointed at Bumble.

"He's quite a mouse. He single-handedly saved our lives you know."

She smiled and answered, "Yes I know. Mine too. Henry's quite an expert at that."

25

The Mouse Clandestine Services

Bumble and Daisy sat in the waiting room outside of the Prime Minister's office at Number 10 Downing Street. A lot had happened in the last six weeks.

Inspector Baxter had been relieved of his duties as Head Mouse and reassigned to the North Pole. Headquarters quickly recognized him as a political operator who cared only about himself. They needed a mouse with courage and character to be in charge, someone who not only understood his fellow mice, but who could also bring them all up higher. And so, Bumble was promoted to Head Mouse, a position he gladly accepted.

Bumble's duties kicked in immediately. He and Daisy had spent the last few weeks touring several Air Transport Command bases, where Bumble had become something of a celebrity, giving advice to the various Tire Tread Task Forces, Leak and Puddle Patrols and Nuts and Bolts Retrieval Units, helping them to operate more effectively.

Crash meanwhile, was promoted to full pilot and given Davenport's quarters. He happily adopted Chief, who became the base's first official mascot. Station 102's accident rating was washed clean, and the base is now the best in the service. Supply flights to neighboring fighter and bomber units all go like clockwork and without a hitch. After some repairs to her hydraulic hoses, *Eightball Charlie* became Station 102's number one plane. The bullet lodged in the port engine did eventually fall out, and was recovered by a member of Nuts and Bolts Retrieval on a routine inspection. No one ever knew how it got there.

Archie returned to the Deception Division and has helped develop several new and brilliant devices along with the Agents, whose codenames continue to change every day and for no real reason.

The biggest changes, however, were saved for the regular working mice at Station 102. Many followed Bumble's example and learned about engine mechanics. They helped the humans greatly by climbing into the smallest and hardest to reach spaces. Anything that needed to be taken apart to fix was now happily assigned to the mice. They helped get the planes back up into the sky in tip-top shape and in record time.

The sound of a buzzer signaled that the Prime Minister was now ready. Daisy squeezed Bumble's hand as they were carried in by one of the Prime Minister's several busy secretaries. The thick padded door opened and inside, sitting behind his large desk, talking on the telephone was Winston Churchill. Wearing his trademark polka-dotted bow tie and puffing on a large and stinky cigar, he looked just like his photos in the newspaper.

The secretary set them on the desk gently and quickly left the room. Bumble remembered the image of Churchill on the "Deserve Victory" poster, and was quite overwhelmed to be here, now, with the man himself. Churchill looked up, saw the mice and clipped the phone conversation short.

"I have to go now. Please remind our esteemed colleague that he cannot shrink away from the challenges that lie ahead. None of us can. Tell him Winston said so! And don't take no for an answer!" and with that he hung up the phone with a loud CLANG. Bumble and Daisy jumped at the noise. Churchill turned to the mice and smiled his big bulldog smile. Bumble and Daisy smiled back. Churchill puffed on his cigar and waited. Bumble and Daisy stood there and tried not to fidget.

An awkward moment passed.

Churchill puffed on his cigar again, leaned in close and whispered in a very secretive manner, "Imagine my surprise…when a little bird told me that mice can, in fact, talk."

Bumble immediately started to sweat, and looked to Daisy. Her eyes grew as big as saucers and she bit her bottom lip. How could he know? What little bird told him? Maybe it was Robin.

Another awkward moment passed. Bumble showed signs of cracking. Churchill gleefully applied a little more pressure.

"Are you silent because you don't know what to say? Or do you choose not to cast your pearls before swine?"

"You're no swine Sir! You're a great man!" Bumble blurted out. Churchill thumped the table in excitement.

"Ha ha! Your first words, and already we agree on something!" Churchill was very pleased. "Have no fear, I shall keep your secret – I can be very discreet when I choose to be."

"Thank you, Sir." Bumble offered up in relief.

"Of course we trust *you* Mister Prime Minister, it's just other people we're not too sure about." Daisy added.

"I don't blame you. I don't know who to trust either."

Bumble and Daisy relaxed. Churchill picked up a file and opened it. He looked at Bumble.

"Henry Humblestone, I presume?"

"Yes, Sir...but everyone calls me Bumble."

Churchill looked at the file and then to Daisy.

"And you must be Marguerite La Fleur. Congratulations on a brilliant achievement."

"Yes Sir, thank you, Sir...but I actually prefer to be called Daisy."

"Hmmm, it seems my file on you two is in need of some updating. Very well. Bumble and Daisy it is. Please be seated."

Churchill dropped the file, moved a pencil box behind them and motioned for them to sit. He didn't waste any time.

"I have three bits of business to discuss with you. This is the first, and the most official."

He opened his desk drawer, reached in and cleared his throat.

"Please stand," he said, and his eyes sparkled mischievously. No sooner had Bumble and Daisy sat down that they now stood right back up again. Churchill continued.

"It is a far more satisfactory endeavor for me to give awards instead of receiving them. And so, I present you with this…"

He pulled his hand from the drawer to reveal The Dickin Medal, a beautiful bronze medallion given to honor the work of animals in war. Pinned on a ribbon of striped green and dark brown, and inscribed with the words "For Gallantry" and "We Also Serve" inside a laurel wreath, it was a spectacular surprise. Bumble gasped when he saw it. Daisy's eyes welled up as she tried to keep herself from crying.

"I'm told we've given twelve of these to pigeons and seven to dogs, but that you are the first mice to ever receive one. There is an inscription on the back that says the following: 'This medal is to be awarded to animals that have displayed *conspicuous gallantry or devotion to duty while serving or associated with a branch of the Armed Forces or Civil Defense Units.'* But to be honest, that seems a bit stiff to me, and I never like reading someone else's words when I can recite my own."

Churchill paused for effect, and cleared his throat.

"And so, I present this to you, Bumble and Daisy, with the certain knowledge that *never has anyone so small accomplished something so big to help so many.*"

He handed them the medal, and they stared at it in amazement. "Would you look at that..." Bumble said softly. Churchill smiled and reached back into his desk drawer to pull out a small piece of parchment paper tied with a red ribbon.

"The second bit of business comes from your fellow mice at the One Hundred and Second Station of Air Transport Command. It seems they are very sorry for their former treatment of you, and out of sincere gratitude for what you have done for them, they have pooled their funds in order to gift you with this..." Churchill handed the parchment to Bumble who opened it and read:

"A lifetime membership to The Cheese Eaters League." Bumble was again stunned. Churchill smiled again.

"It seems you've made them eat their words. Let us hope it gives them some indigestion."

Bumble showed the parchment to Daisy. It was written in very official looking type and even had a seal pressed into the bottom right corner. It looked like a diploma. A lifetime of cheese, how marvelous a thought! Churchill continued.

"Now for the last – and most interesting – bit of business. It is my understanding that the combined efforts of you and a team of fellow creatures resulted in the destruction of the Port-Bail Bridge in France.

"You should know, that was a job assigned to a special commando team – Force 7 from Salisbury – but, thanks to faulty Resistance communication, they were all captured. Not only did you help establish proper communication for the Resistance moving forward...but thanks to your destruction of the bridge, the subsequent interruption of German troop and equipment movement is profoundly significant. Well done!

"Before today, if you were to ask me if I thought any of this 'mousepionage' business would have been possible I would have said no. But the facts speak for themselves. The value of micro-agents out in the field will be of great benefit to us.

"And so, my last bit of business is to offer you both a job. Positions reporting directly to me, in which you, and whatever mice you choose, will undertake missions of all sorts deemed necessary and important to His Majesty's Government. I am, at present, considering calling it *The Mouse Clandestine Services*. What do you think of that?"

It took a moment for it all to sink in. Bumble and Daisy were speechless. Churchill puffed on his cigar and gave it one last push.

"Shall we K-B-O then?" he asked.

"Keep Buggering On?" Bumble replied, repeating Churchill's famous phrase used to boost the public's spirits throughout the war.

"No! Keep Bumble Occupied! Britain needs you both and so do I. If I wanted nothing done, I know many men in Parliament who would be up to the task. But it is now better and necessary, in my estimation, to ask a mouse to do a man's job."

Bumble looked to Daisy who nodded enthusiastically. Bumble squeezed her hand.

"Yes, Mister Prime Minister. I – we – will do it!"

"Of course you will. Splendid! And you'll do a top job of it too, I am sure."

Bumble and Daisy again nodded in agreement as Churchill pulled out a sheet of paper and started reading.

"Now then, it seems there have been reports of gremlins attacking fighters and bombers from the 56th Fighter Group in Halesworth, wreaking all kinds of mechanical havoc. I need you to look into that."

"Gremlins? That's speaking figuratively I hope?"

"Actually no, quite to the contrary. Pilots and mechanics swear they've actually seen the tiny tyrants trying to pull the planes apart in mid-air. Strangest thing I ever heard of. But they can't be very big, so you chaps should be able to handle them."

Bumble gulped. Churchill continued.

"Have you heard of Bletchley Park?" he asked.

"No, Sir."

"We call it *Station X*. It's our code-breaking unit. They've been quite busy lately and will need some of your attention when you get back from Halesworth."

Just then the phone rang, and Churchill sighed. The meeting was over.

"That's enough to get you started. Off you go. I have to take this call. No doubt this is some fresh calamitous news to brighten my day."

And with that, the door opened, and a different secretary than the one before came in and whisked Bumble and

Daisy out of the Prime Minister's office. And just like that, their lives were changed forever.

Bumble and Daisy made their way downstairs and to the street outside, where Chief was waiting for them patiently. He was very excited to hear all about what happened.

Daisy stopped in her tracks.

"Oh dear! We didn't even get a chance to thank Mr. Churchill!" Daisy realized.

"Oh, I think we'll be seeing him again. I think we'll be seeing a lot of him actually." Bumble reassured her.

"How did it go?" Chief asked.

"Oh, it went..." was Bumble's exhausted reply. His mind was swirling.

"It went very well." Daisy added. "You are looking at the heads of newly formed Mouse Clandestine Services. Go on...show him the medal!" Daisy nudged Bumble in the side.

Bumble hefted it up for Chief to see. The Dickin Medal sparkled in the daylight. Chief's eyes went wide. "Woof! That's big! And it's so shiny! But what does it mean?" Chief asked excitedly.

Bumble petted his friend warmly and took Daisy's hand as they walked together into the busy London streets.

What *did* it all mean?

"Well old friend, I think it means we're all going to be busy...very busy indeed."

THE END

Author's Note

T he British did drop forged stamps to the French Resistance. Counterfeit stamps of different financial values all featured one or two secret marks that only the recipient would know to look for. The number of perforations along the sides of the stamp was also unique to the forgeries. Amazingly, the use of these stamps was never discovered, and many can be found today in collections around the world.

The Dickin Medal is a real medal of honor for animals, and was distributed with great frequency until 1949. In October of 2000 it was revived, and its most recent awarding, as of this writing, was in April of 2016 to a German Shepard named Lucca who sniffed out improvised explosive devices in Iraq and Afghanistan. Thirty-two carrier pigeons, thirty dogs, three horses and one cat have received this great honor to date.

The Confidential Pigeon Service was the code name of a British intelligence operation dedicated exclusively to the use of homing pigeons for information gathering. Beginning in 1940, crates of pigeons were regularly parachuted into occupied Europe. The locals would write down anything they thought important (such as German troop movements) on tiny sheets of very thin paper and roll that paper into small tubes attached to the pigeon's legs. When released, the pigeons then did what came naturally, and flew the information straight back to England. The existence of The Confidential Pigeon Service was kept secret until 2007, when Britain's National Archives officially released files relating to its activities.

Eightball Charlie was named after an actual C-47 in active service during the war. The plane carried troops and participated in many important operations from D-Day through VE-Day. The names of the other planes in the story are also real. The code names of the Agents were borrowed from authentic operational code names used throughout the war.

The Cabinet War Rooms in London were renamed The Churchill War Rooms in 2012. The underground bunker is an extremely popular tourist destination. It is a spectacular piece of living history, a place frozen in time, presented to the public exactly as it was left the day the Central Map Room closed on August 16, 1945.

If you wander off the beaten path however, and find yourself at a mysterious door at the farthest end of the longest corridor, we can neither confirm nor deny the existence of anything you might find there...

Bumble Humblestone will return...

Made in the USA
Middletown, DE
18 July 2020